The Little Boy from SoHo

R. E. McKenna

First Edition

PAGE PUBLISHING, INC.
New York, NY

First originally published by Page Publishing, Inc. 2018

This book is a work of fiction. The characters and events in the book are fictitious. Any similarity to real persons living or dead, is coincidental and not intended by the author.

ISBN 978-1-64138-782-8 (Paperback)
ISBN 978-1-64138-784-2 (Digital)

Printed in the United States of America

In Memory of
Captain John J. McKenna IV, USMC
Killed in Action
Iraq
August 16, 2006

To my wife, Diane, who has stood
by me for all these years.
To my daughter Jenn and to my son Rob.

Ellie Buck
Thank you for all your help.

Preface

You wake up during the middle of the night because you are dreaming that you are locked behind a brick wall, stuffed in the trunk of a car, locked inside a refrigerator, trapped inside a cardboard box, in the basement of a crazy's house, on a jet as a sole passenger and you can't get the pilot's attention. You are experiencing reality as you see it in a dream. You are calling out for someone to help you out, out of the situation you are in. You can hear them, they just walk by. No one stops, they are too involved in their own world to enter yours, or maybe, you think they hear you and recognize your voice, but simply refuse to help you by silently walking away. You are seeking help from someone who doesn't want to help you.

You reach a point where *you* must convince yourself that you are the only one who can help *you*. You are having an experience which cannot be explained.

What do you do? Where do you start? You continue to scream, scratch at the wall or the door, fight to cut through your bindings. You look for something that will break you out of wherever you are. Unlock the door, knock down the wall, anything. You fight, you fight and you continue to fight until you ultimately wake up and the dream is over.

That is what happened to me. This story is not a bad dream, but reality. My experiences have convinced me that what everyone is saying is a lie, and no one wants to listen to my story. Sure, a man confessed to a murder, many years after it was committed. People believe him, because they need to have someone to blame. I believe he had nothing to do with the murder.

My story has been told by me to the news media, the defense attorney, and the prosecution lawyers. I have been dismissed by them like a bad dream.

I can't scratch out a result. My screams are not heard, it is not a dream, it is my reality. I cannot wake up from this story until I have told it in its entirety. Now I am telling it to you. You will make a difference—the difference of a man being freed or possibly spending the rest of his life in jail. He made one admission and everyone jumped on it as though he was the Lord preaching a story from the gospel. Yet when there are multiple omissions in this story, the silence is deafening.

You will ultimately make the decision after reading this story. You can convince others that they too need to read this book and help keep an innocent man from being kept in prison for the rest of his life.

1

The First Day at the Law Firm

The streets in New York City during the summer months, especially August, could be very hot, humid, rainy, or gloomy; no one liked any of the options, but somehow people always survived year to year. The law firm of Alcort, Ventura, Johnson, Evans & O'Neill was located on the northwest corner of Broadway and Worth Streets. Just blocks from the infamous "Five Points," a murderous hellhole for Irish immigrants. A federal courthouse now sits on the exact location where the fight from the movie *Gangs of New York* was supposed to have taken place.

The partners had recently purchased the entire five-story building and moved their law office into their new location and they were now close to the criminal, supreme, and federal courthouses. No more waiting for car services. It was now a short walk back to the office from the courthouses. The Attorneys would take a five-star limousine service and bill it back to the client with a profit, when the need occurred.

William Bailey Careswell held tightly to his overstuffed leather carrying case and his "Redweld," as he stood and looked up at the numbers to the building. He stood five feet eight inches, a trim physique, his black hair was neatly trimmed. People crossed in front of him and behind him. He didn't care, he was in New York and it was his first day at the law firm. The donut cart vendor shouted out, "Hey, it's your first day at the firm, come, come over here. I will give you a free cup of coffee to celebrate and do not forget it was Mohammed who first welcomed you to New York City." Careswell stood in silence for a moment as he looked at the man.

"Don't worry, I have been at this location for twelve years, your firm just moved in. I have already given everyone their welcome cup of coffee. It is your turn to get one of Mohammed's welcome cups of coffee."

Careswell walked over to the cart. "I would prefer a cup of tea, I don't really like coffee."

"I don't like bacon with my eggs, so that makes us even," Mohammed said.

Careswell threw a twenty-dollar bill into the cart and walked away with his cup of tea. He stopped and turned back to the cart.

"If I stay, just deduct my morning cup of tea from that twenty. If I come out through those doors running, the twenty is yours," Careswell said and walked into the lobby of the building. Mohammed politely smiled and understood. He had lived in America, mostly New York City, for over twenty-five years.

A security guard greeted Careswell, "Good morning, sir, I need to see your identification card."

"Sorry, this is my first day here, didn't they send down a memo that I would be needing an identification card," Careswell said.

The guard reached over to his clipboard and smiled. "You must be Mr. Careswell."

"Yes, that is me, but you can call me Billy."

The guard looked at Careswell with a strong authoritative look. "Mr. Careswell, if I ever called you by your first name, I would be fired on the spot. I have six kids and a seventh on the way, I need this job."

"Then it is Mr. Careswell."

"I can call you 'sir,' if you would like," the guard said.

"I guess I will need a photo ID," Careswell said.

"Sir, stand on those two stars and look at the camera. I will have your card for you in seven seconds, and you will be on your way. Just remember it is a 'prox' card so just put it near the scanner before you enter. Remember, you must swipe out when you leave the building, for whatever reason, or the system will not let you back in. Your supervisor will have to come down to verify who you are and approve your reentry. Sorry but that is your company's policy."

The guard handed Careswell his new laminated identification which allowed him access to the entire building. The guard walked from behind his desk to show Careswell how to "swipe" his card. Once in, Careswell turned to the guard.

"What is your name?"

"Benjamin Franklin," he replied proudly.

"Mr. President will be the name I'll call you, if that's all right with you."

"Sir, thank you very much," Franklin said and saluted Careswell. Careswell returned the salute.

The elevator reached the fifth floor with the ubiquitous ping, then the doors opened. Careswell was greeted by a bevy of security cameras; he smiled. The large bulletproof glass doors opened slowly, Careswell waited. He approached the receptionist's desk and put his Redweld on top of her desk. The receptionist, a woman in her midthirties, stylish hair, green eyes, wearing a slight coating of lip gloss, rose from her chair and smiled at Careswell.

"Good morning, sir, do you have an appointment with us today?" she asked.

Careswell held out his new ID card for her to read. "I work here."

"I'm sorry, but we do that as a precaution, for safety reasons," she said meekly.

"My name is William Bailey Careswell, but you can call me Billy. Today is my first day at the firm."

"I have to call you Mr. Careswell, it's company policy."

"I understand that. I have an appointment with Mr. Alcort."

She scanned her computer monitor and then picked up the wired telephone and talked quietly.

The receptionist turned to Careswell and held the telephone to her breast. "Mr. Careswell, please have a seat, Mr. Alcort will be with you in a few minutes."

Thirty Minutes Later

"Follow me please," the receptionist said as she stood up from her desk. Careswell closed the folder he had been reading and returned it to his Redweld. He looked at his reflection in the glass door as he followed the receptionist to the large set of doors at the end of the hallway. She knocked politely and partially opened the door. He enjoyed the aroma of her perfume, though he was happily married with two sons, and a daughter on the way. The receptionist turned to Careswell with a professional smile. "Mr. Alcort will see you now."

Careswell quickly walked into the large office, showing his professional look. Mr. Alcort was seated behind a large mahogany desk. He closed the folder he was reading and looked up to Careswell. He waited momentarily, then stood and extended his hand. Careswell gently received it, he tightened his grip as Alcort returned the handshake. They released their grip on each other as Alcort smiled. "I like a man with a firm handshake."

"Did I pass the test?"

Alcort didn't respond but directed Careswell to the chair beside him. "Alcort, Ventura, Johnson, Evans & O'Neill usually selects their candidates from the top three percent of university law students throughout the country. A headhunter, whom I adore, suggested our firm take a look at your resume. I see that you have the case file, I had my service deliver to your house. I hope you had time to read it over," Alcort said.

"I did read the case file three times. It seems it is an open and shut case for the prosecution. The defendant admitted twice to the police that he kidnapped and killed the little Zapata boy. It's a shame, I mean, he killed this little boy, who was on his way to school. It was the first time the boy ever ventured out onto the busy streets of Manhattan, alone. I have two boys. One is the same age as the boy was at the time of his disappearance." Alcort stood up from his chair and walked around his desk.

"We are defense attorneys, not assistants for the prosecution. We are here to defend people." Careswell shifted in his chair, he decided to remain seated.

"I understand, but this guy Fausto Munoz admitted to the police that he took the little boy to the basement of the store and killed him. That was after he made advances toward him. I know there was no body, so no forensic evidence, which would have helped our case, but his confessions can't be discounted."

"I had a feeling you would say that. We have a private law library of all the cases our firm has handled. Some of the cases we won, others didn't end so positively. Pick a few of the old cases and read them. There is one case that is under glass, which I want you to read. You will have to follow the electronic instructions to turn the pages. It was my first case, but do not read it until you have read through at least three other cases."

"Will I be paid for today's work?" Careswell asked.

"Yes, you will, as of today, you are a salaried employee of this firm, welcome aboard." Alcort extended his hand to welcome Careswell to the company.

An Hour Later

Billy Careswell stood in the empty elevator and stared at the floor indicator. His floor would be basement number one or B1, he tightened his grip on his Redweld. The bell didn't ping. He waited for the doors to open.

He stepped out into the large room filled with file cabinets and spotted the illuminated display case. He slowly walked over to it, but suddenly stopped. He turned to a file cabinet and slid out a bottom drawer and removed one of the recent cases of the law firm. He placed it alongside the Munoz case, on one of the seven tables in the room. He wondered why his boss, the senior partner of the firm, had him sit in the basement and read old case files. Suddenly the back door opened and a large tattooed man walked in as he pushed his mop bucket. Careswell smiled, then buried his head into the file. The man continued to approach. His hair was mostly silver with slight black streaks; it is knotted into a ponytail. He wore a small green cap with "Vietnam 1966 to 1972" on the front. Careswell looked up from the files as he closed them over.

"Hey, sorry to interrupt, I'm Larry, the porter for the building. I'm a Nam Vet, as you can tell." He showed Careswell his five battle tattoos.

"Thank you for your service."

"I didn't do it for you. I did it for my neighborhood buddies. Two of them were drafted during the lotteries in the seventies. They went to basic training and were immediately sent to Nam, so I joined them."

"How was it over there?" Careswell asked.

"It sucked. It was hot, no water that you could drink, you took a five-second shower, if you were lucky. Then you walked in water all day so your feet got messed up real bad, if you didn't keep them dry."

"I mean the fighting, was it that real?" Careswell asked.

"I'll put it this way. One day we were attacked by about five hundred North Vietnam regulars. We had no idea where they were coming from, but we kept killing them and they still kept coming. My friends were just teenagers. They never hurt anyone that didn't deserve it. Now they were killing people. I had tossed six grenades in quick succession, expecting them to be returned, but suddenly there was a massive explosion and the ground all around us began to collapse. We had walked right into their living room. They were below ground, right underneath us, like we were tenants on the first floor and they had the basement apartment. Suddenly there was silence. The birds didn't even chirp. I counted our dead. Seventy-five of my guys were dead or near death. The remainder were lying wounded. I, for some reason, was not hit. I thanked my father."

"What happened after that?" Careswell asked.

Larry walked around the table and stared at Careswell. "When I returned home to the states, there were a lot of protesters calling us baby murderers and such. It was hell. There was no support or jobs, so I fell into the wrong group and I got caught doing a robbery. I plead guilty to a grand larceny but later they tried to pin a robbery-murder on me. Man, when I was arrested, I never felt so alone. The woman they said I robbed was eighty-four years old and a grandmother who was supporting her twelve grandchildren on her social security money. I didn't do it, no one believed me, that was until Mr. Alcort came to the holding cell to announce that he was my new attorney. I have been with him ever since. Why are you here?" Larry asked.

"I got this case handed to me because I am the junior guy. I know that, but this was one case that was clearly a no contest. I have to be honest, I am a Christian type of guy, and it is against my faith to lie. There is no way I can say he, Munoz, is innocent, when I actually believe that he is totally guilty. There is no way I can say to a jury that my client didn't murder this little boy, there is no evidence that proves he did it, all they have are his confessions, and he has confessed to murdering the little boy, twice."

"I know that feeling. There are times on the battlefield when a soldier takes his/her own life because of all the drama, issues, and fears. You can't write home to the soldier's parents and say their child was a coward. Their child has to be a hero in their eyes and in yours. God gives us guidance toward those goals, as difficult as they may seem," Larry said.

"This is about the law, not someone's belief in God. It involves a very sensitive issue and could result in some very serious jail time for the defendant, my defendant," Careswell said.

"I'm not going to stand here and preach to you about God. If I don't get those wastepaper baskets emptied, there will be hell to pay. I believe Mr. Alcort made the right selection by bringing you into this law firm," Larry said.

"I'll need to read this file over again," Billy said.

Larry grabbed a can and emptied it into his large Rubbermaid trash container. "Hey, I ain't no lawyer, but I heard enough in the last ten years to know that I can just honestly say, look for something other than the obvious. I gotta go. Hey, by the way, what is your name?"

"Billy, my name is Billy when we talk down here."

"Billy it is. Remember 'free will.' You gotta take your case where it needs to go, the way God would want you to take it."

Larry pressed the button for the elevator and waited, a few seconds later it arrived. He took his large garbage barrel and pulled it into the elevator. The doors closed.

There was absolute silence as Billy spread out his files over the entire table. The air-conditioning unit turned on and the vent over the table blew some of the papers onto the floor. He quickly retrieved them. He looked at the border of one of the pages and thought to himself, *I didn't see this before. I guess the previous defense attorney wanted to erase the name, whomever it was.* He looked closely at the sheet of paper. He gently rubbed his pencil over the back of the sheet of paper. He turned the sheet over and placed a clean sheet of paper underneath the original and began to gently rub the page. He turned the paper over and there was a name and telephone number.

Billy to himself, *Okay, Larry, you said I have free will and that God gave it to me, now I need to use the God-given free will to make this call.*

Larry returned to the basement for more paper recycling bags. "Sorry to interrupt, but I have to get more recycle bags. They just finished another meeting and there is always a ton of paper that needs to be shredded," Larry said.

"I didn't hear the elevator bell ring," Billy remarked.

"I disconnected it a while ago at the request of the lawyers who use this space."

"You don't have to explain to me every time you walk by me."

Larry smiled as he pulled out the large box and removed a handful of clear paper recycling bags. He said to himself, *I do it for myself.*

Billy put the case files on the table and turned to Larry. "You are here for a reason, and I like the idea of free will. Do you know anyone in this office who exercised their free will and are still employed?" Billy asked.

"None that I know of, but I have never been able to talk with the lawyers, or should I say, they never want to talk to me. I believe you are the first."

Billy stood up from the table and walked over to Larry. “How long have you been employed here?”

“Just a little over twenty years.”

“And I’m the first lawyer that has spoken to you.”

“Yeah and no. They do talk to me, like, ‘Hey, Larry, could you get the papers that fell behind my filing cabinet . . .’ Then there is the ‘Hey, Larry, my phone is not working . . . ,’ so I plug it back in the wall. There is always the classic from the new lawyers, ‘Hey, Larry, where can I get laid in this city?’ My response is always, at home.” Billy smiled and returned to the table and began reading.

Two Hours Later

Billy finally mustered up the courage to call the number that was almost obliterated. The phone rang five times. Billy pulled the receiver from his ear, when he heard the faint “Hello.”

“Hi, Lieutenant, I sort of need your help.”

“Why, who is this?”

“My name is William Bailey Careswell, from the law firm of Alcort, Ventura, Johnson, Evans & O’Neill. I have been asked to defend Fausto Munoz on his retrial. His first trial ended in a hung jury.”

“Lucky for him,” the lieutenant said.

“Lieutenant, I saw your name and telephone number on his previous lawyer’s notes. It appeared that the defense attorney didn’t want anyone to have any knowledge of you. Is there anything that you know that could help me defend Mr. Munoz?”

"Did Jim leave any of his interview notes in the file?" the lieutenant asked.

"None, and I have read the entire file."

"Then the previous defense attorney knew I was right. Hey, buddy, with the long name, I need a shorter version of your name."

"Billy, call me Billy."

"Okay, Billy, our interview will have to take some time, do you have that time for me?"

"Lieutenant, we will take all the time we need."

Billy put the phone in the cradle. Eight different scenarios were going through his mind. He walked to the elevator, pressed the call button, then he turned to look in the mirror on the wall. "Let's go to the boss's office and have a chat with him."

Billy waited as the slow elevator ascended to the executive floor. The doors slid back, he stepped into the large reception area, as he held the Redweld containing Munoz's case file. He approached the secretary, but stopped halfway to the desk. "I'll need to see Mr. Alcort . . . immediately."

"He has been waiting for you," the secretary replied. She pointed her index finger at his face. "You did not get that from me."

"I understand."

She pressed her intercom button. "He's here."

"Show him in."

She stepped from behind her desk and walked over to the large mahogany doors. She pushed the door open with relative ease and walked inside, Billy followed. Mr. Alcort was seated at his desk, he looked up from his paperwork, he closed the case file and placed his hand on top of it.

"Mr. Careswell, did you find anything that may help your client, and did you read the other files I asked you to look over?"

"I did, but I would like to discuss the Munoz case first."

"Go on."

"I'm not certain this is as easy a case to prove as most may think. I had my doubts of his innocence, like everyone else. I have asked a lieutenant to come into the office. I want to interview him personally. His name and phone number had been erased from one of the files. I was able to retrieve them, and I called him. He said he was there that first night, I have seen nothing in the case file referencing him to the case and he does remember it clearly, he even has his old police memo book from that night which indicated he was there, and he did search for the little boy."

Alcort returned to his desk and took a deep breath. "Mr. Careswell, I believe you may have stepped in the proverbial pile of crap."

"I hope so."

Alcort got up from his chair. "Let's go into my private office."

"I thought this was your private office," Billy said as he looked around the large office.

Alcort pressed a button under his desk which caused a large bookcase to slide forward slightly and then to the side. The opening was wide enough for two very large men to walk through simultaneously.

The hidden room was surprisingly large for a "Private Office."

"Why the second room?" Billy asked.

"There are times when I need it to get away from everyone, including my secretary. Have a seat at my desk. Go on, it's okay," Alcort said.

Billy sat in the high-back leather chair and stopped. He looked at the picture on the wall opposite the desk. It was a military photo of a young man in his late teens. "Why do you have your janitor's picture on that wall?"

Alcort walked over to the picture and stared at it for a minute. He turned to Billy, "He's my inspiration."

"He's your janitor and an ex-con at that," Billy said.

Alcort smiled and walked away from the picture to sit on a long leather couch. "Did you read the file under the glass, like I suggested?" Alcort said.

"I did skim through it, but if it is that important to you, I will come in early tomorrow morning and read it before my meeting with the lieutenant."

"Many years ago, my father worked for this firm and had a case which everyone thought was a 'no-brainer.' The defendant did it, he murdered an eighty-four-year-old woman, then he raped her and took her money and jewelry. There was some forensic evidence. Forensic science was in its infancy at the time. The woman's jewelry was found under the defendant's mattress. He swore he was innocent and my father took his word for it and the case. It was supposed to be an easy case for the prosecution and it was." Alcort pointed to the picture on the wall. "My father's client, Larry McCormick, was found guilty of murder and sentenced to die. He was the last person executed, ten minutes after the Supreme Court ruled to end executions in New York State. There is no record of the execution."

Billy momentarily closed his eyes and shook his head. "Wait, I'm confused. You have a picture of your janitor on your wall and you are telling me he was your dad's defendant, who has been dead for many years."

Billy got up from the chair and walked over to the picture. Alcort returned to his chair. "I sent you to the basement because you seemed confused, did Larry help you?

"Who the hell was Larry?"

2

Hide and Seek Beth Israel Cemetery, Upstate New York

Thirty-Seven Years Earlier

The light blue 1972 Chevy Malibu with New York license plates was parked at the entrance to the small cemetery which was established in the 1880s. The cast-iron fencing which surrounded the cemetery had been installed forty years earlier to prevent grave desecration. A Jewish philanthropist donated the fencing and a local farmer installed it to supplement his meager earnings from his crops. Two other properties were designated and designed to be exclusively for members of the Jewish faith. Those cemeteries had been licensed in the 1950s, as more elderly members of the Jewish community decided to retire to the many upstate communities. Beth Israel had many of the original trees, which were favorites of some non-Jewish children during Halloween time. Although no real damage had ever occurred, the philanthropist, whose parents were buried in the cemetery, wanted to keep the children from desecrating any tombstones.

The driver of the Chevy stared at the gate. Alan Zapata was a nebbish man, five foot seven, one hundred thirty pounds, his hair was already receding past his ears. He was a public relations / media consultant, as well as a photographer. His consulting business made very little and his photography was in its infancy. A wedding here and there helped to pay the rent. He wanted to purchase a secondhand car preferably without a radio. He hated the rock music that was played constantly on the radio, he preferred the quiet. The music was called the top thirty for each station, and every two and a half hours, the songs were replayed. He never read a newspaper. He listened to WOR710 AM for whatever information he needed. He wore black bell-bottom pants and a floral shirt. His hair was shoulder length, it was matted. His nails were long and dirty. His personal grooming was his last concern. He owned no suits, just jeans and floral shirts. He dropped out of high school after he was spotted taking pictures of girls changing in their locker room. His parents allowed him to stay away from school after the incident, for fear of retaliation. His school record had been expunged as a favor. Now he sat waiting for a distant cousin to help him once again.

Alan Zapata's body suddenly tightened when the headlights of a New York State trooper car neared, the car stopped behind Alan Zapata's car, then the emergency lights came on. The headlights were blinding, but it was the dreaded red roof lights that all motorists hated when they traveled the upstate highways. He didn't know what to do. He borrowed a friend's car for the drive. The car was facing the gate and the trooper's car was directly behind his car. His body began to shake. The trooper approached his car cautiously. "Good morning, sir, are you having a little trouble with your car?" the trooper asked.

"No, sir, I am waiting for my cousin Joshua Levy. He is a rabbi here. It is the second anniversary of my wife's death and I wanted him to say a few prayers over her grave," Alan Zapata said nervously.

"I need to see your driver license and the vehicle registration. We have received numerous calls of a suspicious car at this gate." The trooper was in his early forties, stood six foot four, and was about two hundred and ten pounds with an eighteen-inch neck and thick arms.

"I am sorry, sir. I should have called ahead or had my cousin notify the police that I would be arriving early. I have to do this early and then rush home to my job. My boss does not accept a cemetery visit as an excuse for lateness. I wanted to make this visit on this date, because it would have been our tenth wedding anniversary," Alan said as he handed the trooper his driver license and the vehicle registration.

"Oh, I am sorry, sir, which anniversary was it of your wife's death, did you say?"

"My wife died two years ago, today, on our wedding anniversary. I miss her so much."

"Any children?" the trooper inquired.

Alan Zapata immediately recognized the questioning. "No, we had none. She, my wife, became ill almost immediately after we were married. Then she was diagnosed with MS."

The trooper returned Alan's ID to him. "I understand, sir."

Alan sensed that he had the trooper's sympathy. "Thank you, Officer. Is it okay for me to stay here until my cousin comes?"

"Does your friend, er, what's his name, the vehicle's owner, does he know you are here?"

"Chaim Bieber and I are like cousins. I have a lot of cousins in New York."

"I will call it in so we can disregard any more calls for a suspicious car at the cemetery."

"Thank you, Officer," Alan said.

"Call us troopers, the NYPD are called officers," the trooper said, tipped his hat, and smiled. "Have a nice day, sir."

Alan Zapata's heart must have been beating at two hundred times a minute during that conversation. His brow was wet, as was his shirt. He took out a handkerchief after the trooper left the area and wiped his brow. He had run-ins with the NYPD but never with a massive state trooper. He was happy it was over. Now he simply had to wait for his cousin.

"Come on, Joshua, let's get this over with," Alan said as he looked at the gates.

Suddenly a man appeared out of nowhere. The gates suddenly began to open. It was Joshua Levy, he walked over to Alan's car. "I didn't think you would get here this early," Levy said.

Alan was angry, not with the flippant attitude of his cousin, but with the trooper questioning him. "I said I wanted to do this as early as possible. Can I leave him with you?" Alan asked meekly.

"Yes. I would prefer that you prayed for your son alongside him. When the prayers are over, you can put him in my truck and I will take care of the rest," Levy said.

"Thank you," Alan replied. He lifted the trunk lid of his car and placed his hand over Nate's head and prayed. Levy opened the back of his covered pickup truck. Alan carried the thick plastic bags to Levy's truck and placed them into the bed of the truck.

"Now go and be with your wife," Levy said.

Alan handed his cousin an envelope and walked back to his car. He turned to his cousin, "Remember, no matter what you hear or read, say nothing."

"I have done this before, it is you I worry about," Levy said softly. He put the envelope into the jacket pocket of his black suit.

Later That Morning

The narrow road allowed the farmer access to his fields from two sides of the road. It was also an ideal lover's lane. It was unknown to most of the residents of the county, but Rachael had dated the farmer's son discretely. Her father would have thrown her out of the family if he found out she had a non-Jewish boyfriend. She had met Alan Zapata one day while he was taking wedding pictures of a newly married couple. The groom was seventeen years old and the bride was fifteen and very pregnant. She caught his attention when she went up and kissed the bride, after all, they had been classmates for two years. When he completed taking his pictures, he asked her if she would pose for him. She had long auburn hair with slight curls, a couple of freckles accentuated her deep blue eyes. She was five foot six with a long slender body for a young teenager. It didn't take long for the professional photographer to have his way with her. She became pregnant and extremely nervous when she started to show. He took her to a friend whose office was in upper Manhattan. He was a professional at correcting the condition, although it was still illegal. She could never have children after the procedure. She didn't care, she didn't want to be pregnant. Her primary duties were to care for her elderly father who suffered from dementia. Her house had key locks on both sides (of all the exterior doors and all the windows) so he couldn't walk out of the house when she was not home. She had an access valve to shut off the propane tank. He would sit in his rocking chair the entire time listening to his radio. He was happy.

Alan's pants and briefs were around his ankles. Rachael was busy, he was eyeing his watch. "That's what I call role reversal," she said.

"What do you mean?" he moaned.

"I'm doing all the work and you are lying there checking the time." She pulled away and sat on his legs. "Don't tell me you want to be with your wife. She never does this for you."

"Maybe this was a wrong time to be with you," he moaned.

"I can stop."

"No, continue, please."

Rachael moved to continue but hesitated. "Then we go shopping. I need things, a lot of things."

Alan was frustrated and unconsciously turned to look at his watch.

"Do that one more time and you can finish this yourself," she said angrily.

"Okay, all right, just do it and let me finish. I promise I will take you shopping."

"I want lunch also."

"Okay, just finish," he said.

"Hey, you called me at the last minute. Now show me you still have it."

3

As It Was . . .

Alan knew his wife would be worrying, it was already four thirty in the afternoon and he just crossed Fourteenth Street. He would have to fight his way south on Varick Street, which was always backed up to Houston Street every evening at this time. This was also a Friday before a long holiday weekend. He did remember to fill the car with gas in New Jersey, it was much cheaper there than in Manhattan. His afternoon tryst cost him more money than he had expected. Luckily he paid all the bills with checks and controlled their checking account. He could hide Rachael's purchases when the checks cleared and sent to his address. He would destroy the evidence; Rachael would now be history. He suddenly turned left onto Fourteenth Street. It was not crowded. Two blocks and he turned right onto Fifth Avenue. He could see the Arch at the foot of Fifth Avenue at the north side of Washington Square Park. The pill, pot, and other crazy drug dealers had made their way to Washington Square North and hid under the cover of the trees in the park. Alan waited for the light to turn green before he drove past the seven Rastafarians who simulated smoking marijuana by putting their thumb and forefinger together and moving them to their mouth and then pulling their fingers from their mouth. He needed a clear head and he avoided eye contact with his favorite dealer. He pressed the gas pedal which got him quickly to the corner of Washington Square North / Waverly Place and Washington Square West. He turned left onto MacDougal Street / Washington Square West which was quiet, except for a couple of heroin dealers. The traffic light changed at West Fourth Street and MacDougal Street. Alan continued south, he had a clear view of the two World Trade Center buildings in the background. He turned left onto Houston Street and over to West Broadway where he made a right turn for two blocks. The car's owner had a monthly parking space in the garage which formerly housed horses before cars had been invented. Alan put the car in the temp spot and locked the doors. The attendant would retrieve his set of keys to the car and put it in the owner's designated parking spot.

Alan returned the car keys to his friend along with a bottle of Scotch.

The Zapata's apartment house was a converted factory. Their apartment was large, with moveable tall room dividers. Alan knew he would have to keep his son Nate's "area" as it was for a long while. The halls and stairways were sturdy and wide, though the slightest loud argument could be enjoyed by all. The thick concrete floors allowed for children to run around and play without disturbing the neighbors below. There was always someone playing a Jimmie Hendrix album somewhere in the building. Allen adjusted his belt and tucked in his shirt. He didn't want anything to distract his thoughts. He needed for his plan to work. He pulled out his two house keys as he approached the front door to his apartment. He checked for the toothpick he had inserted into the doorjamb when he left. It was still there. *She didn't leave, that is good,* he thought to himself. He rapped five times on the door before unlocking the door and opening it into the apartment. His wife, Arlene, was sitting at the table, her elbows were on the top of the table and her hands held a kitchen towel. She turned to him. Her eyes were red and bloodshot; she had been crying all day.

"I thought you were just dropping off Nate, then coming straight home to be with me," she said.

"I had to wait with my cousin until Nate was covered. I do not trust those people, but it was an emergency, and they were the only people I could think of who would help us. They are almost family," he said softly. He leaned over and held her. She sniffed his shirt, there was no odor of perfume. She pulled him closer, no perfume in his hair. She relaxed and pushed him aside. She stood up and walked over to the sink and cupped her hands to put cold water on her face. She wanted to appear anxious and hopeful, not thinking the worst for her son. She finished and dried off her face and went back to the table, where Alan was now sitting.

"Did you eat anything?" she asked.

"I grabbed a dirty water dog from a cart when I got into Manhattan. How about you?" he said.

"I can't eat, I miss my son so much."

"Let's go over the plan one more time before I call the police."

"I think we should call them now, it is getting late," she said.

"We agreed that we would wait until four but it is five thirty, another half hour will not hurt," he said. He got up from the chair and nervously paced around the open kitchen area. "At six o'clock we call the police, your cousin has been paid and she will lie for us," Alan said confidently.

"I don't trust Sophie, though she is my cousin. What happens when the money runs out or she gets arrested? She could expose us," Arlene blurted nervously.

"I got her so stoned last night that she'll remember nothing. I showed her Nate's body and told her that she killed him in a fit of rage. I told her he wanted to expose her," Alan said. "You killed Nate, you hit him and you killed him."

Alan walked over to his wife and held her tightly, he felt her body relax. "If anything happens, Sophie believes she killed our son. I will deny any responsibility or anything to do with the disappearance of Nate. We know where he is but she doesn't," Alan blurted out. Arlene buried her head in her husband's chest. "But you killed our son."

It took Alan a while to calm his wife. She moved her head away from the comfort of her husband and looked into his eyes. "Will I have to be interviewed by the police?"

"Not if you don't want to be interviewed. You'll portray the grieving mother, just do not talk to any uniformed officers. Some of them can be friendly, helpful, and caring, but they just act that way to make you say something, anything so they can become detectives."

"I will try, but I miss my son."

Alan took a step to her and embraced and kissed her, he moved back slightly. "Stay strong."

4

Staying the Course First Police Precinct, Manhattan 6:10 PM

The muster room of the precinct, which was located in front of the "DESK," had quieted down after the day tour left for home and the four by midnight got their radios and cars for the night. To the civilian or rookie, the change could be challenging, but as with anything else in the police department, you got accustomed to it. The desk sergeant loved this time, it was his/her time to put on a fresh pot of coffee. The initial paperwork had been completed, property which had been vouchered was accounted for, prisoners had been checked, next he would have to wait for anything unusual to happen.

It was a Friday night, which would mean that he'd be long on his way home or to his neighborhood bar, before the craziness started. Friday night was a time to escape for the out-of-state workers. Those coming into the First Precinct were there to park their cars and walk the distance to the clubs in the Sixth Precinct, the Greenwich Village Precinct. In 1979, there was only a single person living in the northwest area of the First Precinct. It ran from Canal Street on the north, south on Broadway to the Battery, and everything to the west from the Battery to Canal Street. The entire area except for the station house was flat barren ground or empty buildings waiting to be razed. The city had a plan for the World Trade Center Area Development. Everyone, who occupied a daytime space in the First Precinct, was a transient, except for a solitary sixty-something-year-old man. There was no need for the NSU I to be working nights, no one was there. Therefore, they worked business hours. NSU II, on the other hand, had been strategically placed to monitor the nightlife in and around Greenwich Village. The Village had been a meeting place since the 1940s. Thousands made their way to the bars on Friday and Saturday nights. Some of the more famous bars were The Back Fence, The Red Garter, Your Father's Mustache, The Bitter End, The Café au Go Go, Café Wa, Folk City, The Bottom Line, Night Owl, Village Gate, just to name a few.

The people came from New Jersey, upstate New York, teenage girls climbed out of their second-story bedroom windows on Long Island, took a train to Manhattan, then made their way down to Greenwich Village. People came to the Village to see the beatniks, who later evolved into the hippies and their counter culture. The coffee shops had their poets, folk song singers like Bob Dylan, and others. It was a cautious peaceful time. Washington Square Park and its denizen of drug dealing and drug use was always lurking to the north. NSU II cops were ordered not to go into Washington Square Park, as it was too dangerous.

First Police Precinct

The switchboard operator handed the desk sergeant back his copy of the roll call, she had copied all the changes onto her copy. The desk phone had been quiet for most of the start of the tour. As usual, when all was calm, the phone would ring. Lydia Ortiz took the call. "First Precinct, PAA Ortiz." There was a pause on the phone as Arlene composed herself. "Yeah, er, hi, er, my son, he didn't come home after school today. I don't know where he is. He is normally home with us right now doing his homework," she blurted. Alan held her hand.

Lydia Ortiz married a cop when she was twenty-one, three months later she became pregnant, and nine months later she had a son. Ortiz's husband was an Irishman, first-generation American. Daniel Gerard Keenan and his wife had agreed to let her keep her maiden name after they married. Five months into their marriage, he had a brain aneurism while working. He died that night. The police department was very good to her, and the camaraderie was something she had never experienced. They helped her through her pregnancy, delivery, and the first year of raising her son, but she needed a job to pay the rent and support her son, Danny Jr. She decided to take the test to become a police administrative assistant. The cops took her to the precinct to see what the job required. She sat with the PAAs and discussed their duties as they worked. She scored top of the list. She was offered a job at One Police Plaza but she wanted to work with the family she knew, the cops of the First Precinct.

"Your name, ma'am."

"Arlene Zapata, why?"

"I need it for my officers, they will need to know who they should ask for when they go to your house."

"Oh, we don't live in a house, we rent an apartment," Arlene said.

"Has your son ever been late before?"

"No, er, today was the first time he went to school by himself. We, I mean my husband and I agreed to let him go to school alone. He had been begging us for weeks. We agreed that he could go to his school by school bus and come home alone by school bus." She finally looked at the script Alan had written for her.

"Ma'am, how old is your son?"

"Nate turned six, two months ago," Arlene said.

Ortiz wanted to scream into the phone but simply thought, *Lady, are you freaking real? Your son is only six years old and you let him go to school alone in Manhattan, really*?

"Ma'am, have you called your son's school?"

"Yes, a few times, but no one is answering the telephone," Arlene said.

"I'll send a car to your home to take a report and do a preliminary investigation. That is procedure. It will be up to the officers to determine if the detectives need to respond and do a search." Ortiz knew to have the sergeant alerted to the situation. It would ultimately be his decision to do a search and to call for additional officers.

"Okay, I will discuss that with my husband," Arlene responded, way too relaxed for Ortiz's ears. Arlene held the telephone for a moment, then looked to her husband.

"Did I do all right?"

"Yes, now we have to wait for the police officers to arrive. I want you to look worried, like you still don't know what happened to our son," he said coldly.

"I will try," Arlene said softly.

"I'll need you to look like you are still looking for Nate. It is only going to be for a while. As long as the detectives are here. Once they are gone, we can try to live a normal life," he said.

"I can't believe that I don't feel more sorrow for the loss of our son," she replied.

"If he told his teacher as he said he would, we would be in jail right now," Alan said cautiously, reminding her of the consequences of what Nate would have said.

"I know, I will do my best." She walked away from her husband and walked into their small bathroom. She closed the lid on the toilet, sat down, and cried until her husband called for her. She looked into the mirror and smiled at her reddened eyes and messed hair. She now looked the part of a distraught mother of a missing son.

Five Minutes Later

Alan heard the three raps on the apartment door and stood up from the couch, a secondhand purchase from Goodwill. A thin bedsheet with stains covered it. He tugged on his belt to raise his pants then pulled down on his polo shirt. His nails were dirty and was his hair. He hadn't shaved in three days, about the same amount of time since his last shower and change of underwear. He checked his photography equipment in case the officers needed a photo of his son, it was pristine.

Alan approached the door as two young uniformed officers waited in the hallway. The officers heard footsteps and stepped to the side of the door for their safety.

The single number 1 collar brass shone in the dim light of the hallway. Alan turned the doorknob. Both officers placed their shooting hand on their weapon and slid their thumb between the revolver and the strip of leather which held it in place to unlock their revolver. Alan opened the door and took a step to the officers, he smiled. The officers pushed their .38 Smith and Wesson revolvers back down into their leather holsters.

The taller officer began. “Good evening, sir, I am Officer Steve O’Halloran and this is my partner Officer Dan Heinz. We’re here about your call to the precinct regarding your son.”

Arlene stepped to the door and stood behind her husband. “Yes, yes, come in, Officers. Our son, excuse me, this is my husband Alan Zapata. Our son Nate went to school today for the first time on his own and he has not returned home,” she blurted, much to the anger of Alan. He did a good job at masking his displeasure with his wife’s intervention.

“Ma’am, can we take a look around your apartment first?” O’Halloren said.

“When are the detectives coming?” Alan interrupted.

“When I get all the information for the report. Now let’s go inside and take a look around the apartment,” O’Halloren said. His partner allowed him to take the lead on this one.

“Our son went to school and failed to return. What else do you need?” Alan said as he tried to control his anger. Arlene wrapped her arms around her husband’s waist.

“Dear, we have to let the officers do their jobs,” she said

“I want the detectives here right now,” Alan blurted.

"I am sorry, sir, but the precinct has only one detective team working today and they are on another call. Once we finish here, I will call my sergeant," O'Halloren explained.

"I want the detectives now," Alan repeated.

"Dear, the officers have to follow their protocols," Arlene whispered but loud enough to please both officers.

"I don't give a damn about their protocols, I want the detectives here now to find our son."

O'Halloren walked through the open spaces of the apartment. He opened and closed doors and looked behind curtains and under raised bedding. Then he turned over all the bedding.

"Just checking," O'Halloren said.

"Honey, I can remake the bed for Nate when he returns, they are only doing their jobs."

"Mr. Zapata, I will need some more information to fill out this missing person report while my partner continues to look for your son," Officer Heinz said as he slid the missing person report under the clip of his clipboard.

"Officer, is it really necessary to destroy my apartment to look for my son when we both know he didn't return home from school today?" Alan said.

"Before I came on the police department, I would have asked that same question. I am here in the First for six years, and we do not have that many families living in here SoHo, but I have responded with my partner to over eight missing child reports. In every case, my partner or I have found the missing child. He has a knack for finding kids. If anyone is going to find your son, it will be my partner," Heinz said.

Alan Zapata knew better.

Later

Officer O'Halloren stood by the street door to the converted factory. He thought to himself about growing up in a building with such a cold atmosphere. The ceilings were very high and the plumbing overhead was exposed. He recently married his girlfriend of just ten months. She was due to deliver their baby soon. They lived in Park Slope which had taken a turn for the worse, but the rents were affordable for the young couple. Her mother lived one floor up from them. She would help babysitting when his wife went back to work. He took all the available overtime to save up enough money for a down payment on a house on Staten Island. Most of the cops he worked with came from Staten Island. Owning a house there would mean he could car-pool with some of the guys in his squad. That made him a little more comfortable about leaving his old Brooklyn neighborhood where he grew up.

The blue-and-white patrol car slowed. O'Halloren stepped from the doorway to meet his sergeant. O'Halloran saluted. "Hey, Sarge, sorry to bother you but it looks like we got a missing six-year-old boy. The parents say they allowed their kid to go to his bus stop alone this morning but the kid did not return home."

Sergeant Zink turned to his driver. "Get another car here or at least a foot cop. I want someone to stay with the parents."

"You got it, boss," the officer said.

"Stay with the car, but stand outside, or lean against the fender, in case the kid decides to show up. If he does, you bring him up to his parents. Then you'll get the cop of the month award," Zink said to his driver.

Zink didn't like taking elevators, instead opted for the stairs. He rode his bicycle into work every day. He lived in West Brighton, Staten Island, and rode his bicycle to the Staten Island Ferry Terminal, where he took the ferry to the Whitehall terminal. Once off the ferry, he rode his bicycle along West Street, which was under the West Side Highway, and rode it to the First Precinct Station house.

Sergeant Zink saw Officer Heinz standing at the edge of the doorway to the apartment, it was open. He was pleased to have experienced officers at the scene, rookies would allow the family to close the door and do whatever they wanted, outside the eye of the police. If a crime had been committed in the apartment, Zink didn't want any evidence destroyed. He removed his uniform eight-point hat and held it under his nonshooting arm as he approached the apartment.

Alan Zapata smirked as he looked at the uniformed sergeant. "I wanted the detectives to find my son," he said.

"Sir, I do not know your name and you do not know mine. I am Sergeant Robert Zink of the First Precinct. I am the patrol supervisor, and as such, I make the call for the detectives to respond here."

"Then make the damn call already," Alan shouted.

Zink was an eighteen-year veteran of the NYPD and had worked in many precincts before he found his home in the First. Zink said calmly, "Sir, can you please tell me how it came to be that you allowed your six-year-old son to take a school bus alone for the first time unsupervised? I know this neighborhood and some of the people who live here. You allowed a six-year-old boy to take a block and a half walk to his bus stop without anyone watching?" Zink asked.

"My wife walked him down to the end of the street and watched him until he was standing in his school bus stop."

"Where was your wife standing in relation to your son?" Zink asked.

"She said she was directly across the street from where he was standing, and she smiled and waved good-bye to Nate when he saw his bus. When the bus left, my son was not there, so my wife assumed he had gotten on the bus with his fellow students."

Zink knew from experience that the traffic along West Broadway was usually backed up for blocks in the morning. It was a one-lane road north bound and one south bound, with "truck parking only" at the curb in the morning to expedite deliveries. It would be impossible for Arlene Zapata to have constant visual contact of her son. He kept that to himself.

Zink circled his wagons as he stood with his officers, out of earshot of the Zapatas. "Give me your gut feelings on this one."

O'Halloren walked away from the doorway, Zink and Heinz followed. "Sarge, I've gone through the subject's building and the adjoining buildings, there is nothing. These buildings give me the creeps. I have enough time on the job to know what to expect when I walk through the halls of these buildings. I still get the heebie-jeebies when I have to knock on a door. Every apartment is occupied by some sort of pervert."

"My wife is a public school teacher and gave me a list of all the school's principals and their direct office and home numbers, just in case I should need them. I think this is the perfect time to use the list," Zink said. It would be a long night. He called the borough and requested the duty captain to respond.

Detective Squad Room

A lone detective scanned the Chinese takeout menu as the telephone began to ring. "First Precinct detectives, Detective Carlson, how can I help you."

"Hey, Vinnie, it's me Richie Alpert, at the desk, is your sergeant available?"

"Sorry, Sarge, he's in the crapper, he got the—"

"Never mind, have him call me at the desk when he pulls himself together. It's somewhat important," the desk sergeant said. "Ten-four, Sarge. I'll let him know."

Carlson rapped on the bathroom door three times. Then he opened the door slightly. "Hey, Sarge, the desk wants you to call him forthwith."

Sergeant Thomas Lawrence sat in disgust at his situation and screamed. "Why the hell does he have to pick tonight to call me with a 'forthwith'?"

Carlson took a step back. "Sarge, I'm only the messenger."

"Vin, get a cop to take the desk and have Sergeant Alpert come up here so I can find out what he wants, thanks. Oh god, here goes another one," Lawrence moaned.

The Desk

Det. Carlson walked to the left side of the desk. "Hey Sarge, Lawrence asked me to watch the desk for. He can't come down here right now, so he'll need you to go up to the squad room, if you know what I mean," Carlson said.

"Okay, sign into the log as being present on the desk but nothing else. If anything comes up and I am still in the Squad room, write it on a sheet of scrap paper and I will make the entry later," Alpert said. "Got it boss," Carlson said proudly. Alpert walked from behind the desk as Carlson made his way up the single step and walked to the center. It was his first time behind a Precinct Desk. The large thick green matting covered the command log lay opened in the center of the desk. Every important event or issue was entered into the log to be held as a record forever. Carlson picked up the ruler and signed his name as being present at the desk, covering for the Sergeant.

Always the Bearer of Bad News.

Sergeant Alpert, a third-generation NYC police officer, was the only family member to achieve the rank of sergeant. His driver license had him at six feet three inches tall, but the constant work behind a precinct desk had made the line on the wall come down a little. His glasses sat comfortably on his head. He was the rare case where a sergeant preferred working behind the desk rather than being on patrol. A patrol supervisor had tremendous freedom on the outside, but it also came with being responsible for the actions of their subordinates.

Alpert looked around the squad room, it was empty but the bathroom door was closed. He tapped on the well-worn door.

"Hey, Tommy, I gotta tell you this. We've have a missing six-year-old," Alpert said.

The bathroom door opened an inch. "How long has the kid been missing?" Lawrence asked.

"Since about zero seven forty-five hours. That is when the mother says she last saw her son as he stood in the bus stop."

"Those 'mothers' on the day tour held this until the end of their tour," Lawrence shouted.

"The TS only got the call from the missing boy's mother at ten minutes after six," Alpert said.

Lawrence looked at his watch. "A half hour ago."

He stepped out of the stall and finished adjusting his belt. "Never on a good day does this happen, only when I got the runs."

"Hey, Tommy, I gotta go, I'll give you some privacy."

"Give Vin Carlson a copy of the sixty-one. Have him go visit the mother. I'll catch up with him later," Lawrence said.

Vin Carlson was the senior detective in the First Precinct, having served twelve years as detective first grade. He was the "go-to guy" for every cop on patrol. He never dismissed a cop's arrest. To him, every arrest was a good arrest, no matter how insignificant it appeared to be. His wife of eighteen years, Toni Ann, handed him divorce papers three weeks earlier, and he had been using the squad dormitory as his own bedroom ever since. His clothes, always pressed and neat, were now dirty and disheveled. The two photos of his teenage girls, Kathryn and Emily, still adorned his desk, sans their mother's half of the photo standing alongside them at their high school graduations. He had never forgotten about the promise they each made each other eight years earlier. They would stay married until both girls graduated high school.

Those eight years, as Carlson put it, was living hell. His younger daughter Emily sensed the anger between her parents.

She wasn't surprised when she, her sister, and her parents went out to dinner to celebrate Emily's graduation from St. Joseph's High School, and Toni Ann handed her husband the divorce papers. The girls helped their father pack his clothes as neatly as possible. Kathryn, cried the entire night.

Sergeant Alpert walked into the muster room and smiled as Carlson stood behind the desk with a ruler in his hand and waited to make his second entry in the Command Log.

"Hey, Vin, your boss is having one of his days, he wants you to read over this scratch copy of the sixty-one. We have a missing six-year-old boy," Alpert said.

Vin Carlson grabbed the copy of the sixty-one and began to read it.

"What the hell time did this kid get out of school?"

Carlson looked at his watch to make his second entry in the Command Log. *1850 hrs, Det. Carlson off desk.* He took the ruler and placed it under the sentence and drew a line across the width of the page, tossed the ruler into the crease of the book and picked up the written copy of the complaint report about the little boy.

5

It All Began Here Outside the Zapatas Apartment House 8:30 P.M.

Vin Carlson held the copy of the UF 61 and conferred with Sergeant Zink. Sergeant Lawrence pulled his unmarked car to the curb. He stepped out of the car and walked over to Zink.

"Bob, got anything more on the kid?"

"This kid may not have been on the school bus in the first place, but let's go talk with the parents," Zink said as they walked through the opened apartment house door. Zink decided to run up the flight of stairs to the Zapatas' floor instead of taking the elevator.

The elevator stopped and the doors slowly opened. Carlson and Lawrence stepped out and were met by Zink, who motioned for the uniformed officer at the door to inform Nate Zapata's parents the detectives had arrived. Alan Zapata jumped up from his chair in front of his photography equipment and stepped quickly to the door. "Finally, the detectives have arrived."

Sergeant Lawrence held out his hand, but neither parent reached to grab it. Lawrence put the complaint report into his empty hand. “It’s busy out here tonight, sorry if we were delayed. Mr. and Mrs. Zapata, I have the officer’s report here. Could you tell me what happened this morning?” he asked.

Arlene was first to respond. “Well, Nate, our son, had been pestering us for over a month to allow him to go and take the school bus by himself. Alan and I had talked it over last night and we decided that we would let our son go to the bus stop alone.”

“By himself?” Carlson asked.

“That’s what alone means,” Alan said coldly.

“Yes, but I did follow him as he walked to the school bus stop. He never turned around. He walked straight to the corner and waited for the light to turn green for him to cross. I was so proud of him,” Arlene said softly. “He stood with the other boys and girls who were waiting with their parents. The bus came, and he got on and it went down West Broadway,” she said

“Mrs. Zapata, where were you when the school bus came to pick up your son and the other children at the bus stop? Did you ever see Nate actually get on the bus?” Carlson asked.

“Well, no, now that you ask. I was standing across the street, behind a tree and the school bus blocked my view. When it left, Nate was not there, so I figured he got on the bus. Why do you ask?”

Sergeant Lawrence looked into Arlene’s eyes but got interrupted by her husband. “Is there a problem here, Detective?” Alan said loudly.

It would have been Sergeant Lawrence's one chance to see if Arlene was lying. Sergeant Lawrence turned to Alan. "Your son was marked absent from school today."

"How do you know Nate was marked absent?" Alan asked, then he looked at the floor.

"I called the principal at his home and asked him to meet one of my officers at his school or send a representative to help the officers. They checked the attendance records. Nate had been marked absent . . . all day," Zink said.

"Well, maybe the school bus driver knows where Nate is," Alan said coldly.

"Officers have been sent to his house to interview him."

"I want to know what happened to my son, I have a right to know," Alan said.

"This search is a preliminary one. There will be more officers responding to help with the canvass of the area. I will have Detective Carlson remain with you for a while. A uniformed officer will remain outside your apartment temporarily."

"Look, I know you fellas mean well, but these people, the residents are different. I would prefer if you stayed away from my apartment door," Alan said.

"If you would like, I could assign an officer to remain inside your apartment until we either find your son or call off the search until daylight," Zink said.

"I definitely don't want an officer in my home for any period of time. As it is now, I will have to answer a million questions in the morning," Alan said nervously.

Detective Carlson walked over to the sergeant and the boy's father. He looked at Alan Zapata. "Do you have any pictures of your son that I can distribute to the officers to help with the search?"

"I am a commercial photographer. I can make up some pictures for your officers."

"That would be a big help," Carlson said.

Sixth Precinct
MacDougal Street
1900 Hours

Officer Bob Joyce had driven his Honda Hawk 400cc motorcycle through the Friday evening traffic, a Friday before another long Memorial Day weekend and the unofficial start of summer. NYU's commencement had been held three weeks earlier and few students remained in the dorms. The drug dealers from the park walked up and down MacDougal Street, until they spotted the uniformed officers. They knew Officer Joyce would be walking the street the entire night, so they drifted toward Sixth Avenue. Joyce stood six feet two inches tall, deep blue eyes, an arresting smile. He was training for the NYC Marathon and enjoyed walking his foot post for further exercise. He and over five thousand police officers had been laid off at midnight June first 1975. He did odd jobs, worked as a bank investigator until an ideal job came up. Former New York Governor, Nelson A. Rockefeller, would be leaving the office of Vice President of the United States and his family security detail consisting of former Secret Service Agents was looking for a New York City cop to join their detail. Joyce submitted his resume and two days later he got the call that he had been selected. He traveled with the former Vice President all over the world until he received the telephone call that he and a thousand laid off police officers would be recalled for active Police duty. He thanked the former U.S. Vice President for the time he served and rejoined his family of police officers. The recall was the largest ever for the Police Department so a plan had been formulated to put the officers into individual units according to the command structure. He and eleven other officers were assigned to a command known as NSU II. They "turned out" of the thirteenth precinct stationhouse, because it was their dedicated precinct, in their division.

That division, also known as the Twentieth Division, encompassed the Sixth, Tenth, and Thirteenth Police Precincts. NSU II had to be mobile on a moment's notice. They were assigned a prisoner van for the evening tours. The box van was used during the daytime to transport prisoners from each of eleven precincts in Manhattan south to court. The prisoners were comprised of drunks, prostitutes, and anyone else who had the misfortune to be charged with a non-serious felony or serious misdemeanor. The vans were never washed, cleaned, fumigated, deloused, nothing. The condition of the interior of the van, when the officers entered, was the same as it was, when the last dirty, smelly prisoner walked out of it earlier that day.

The Village sidewalks were already crowded with tourists, lovers, and the curious. Joyce walked his post, which was on MacDougal Street, between Bleecker Street and West Third Street. He liked the nightlife, he was able to talk with the store owners. They always welcomed the NSU II officer into their stores. Gus had the

Gyro and grill spot on MacDougal Street just north of Bleecker Street. Maria and Carol had the small grocery and newsstand in the middle of the block next to Gus's place. There were four corner coffee shops with outdoor seating. Passerby could hear the musicians playing their songs from the sidewalks. Cars were forever lined up to get to Bleecker Street as there was no parking along both sides of MacDougal Street. Though Joyce walked in the street, he walked close to the curb. The one thing he didn't like was the fact that some of the people walking on the sidewalks did appear taller than he was.

Joyce walked in the street which allowed him a look inside the moving vehicles. He made plenty of arrests for drugs that were in plain view on the front seats or on the raised portion of the floor.

Gus was a second-generation Greek restaurant owner. Though his grill was small, his heart was big. He and Joyce always talked on slow evenings. Their topic of conversation was always about why the officers assigned to the Village had to leave the streets to go to a different area to help out there. It was the same complaint made by many of the store owners. Joyce calmed their fears this night by reminding them it was the start of the Memorial Day weekend and many people were headed out of town. He and Gus would talk for a few minutes as Joyce stood at the entrance of his restaurant. It was Joyce's way of reassuring the store owner's fears—the fear that the drug dealers would take over the streets outside their restaurants.

Suddenly Joyce and the other members of the NSU II received the call, they were mobilized and ordered to report to their van immediately. They were a team and responded to each incident as a team. They entered the van without saying a word, they sat and waited. The sergeant arrived and told them they were going to SoHo to look for a missing boy. No name, description, no vitals, nothing.

West Broadway and Spring Street
2200 Hours

The Neighborhood Stabilization Unit #2 of Manhattan South had mobilized to the northwest corner of Spring Street and West Broadway located in the First Precinct. The twelve officers entered the grocery store (bodega) to get their instructions from their sergeant, but the store owner turned them away. They had to line up outside of the bodega at the curb. Some were given assignments by their sergeants, Gregory and Jaffee.

Detective Carlson and three other detectives met with Sergeant Gregory. He selected four uniformed officers to accompany the detectives as they canvassed the surrounding buildings for information. The remaining uniformed officers stood at the curb as not to interfere with the Friday night pedestrian traffic.

"Hey, Joyce, I'm finally taller than you right now, with you standing down at the curb," a female voice said. The other officers looked over to the six-foot-two-inch-tall cop, who had been given a copy of Nate Zapata's picture. Joyce walked to the street and waited for the traffic light to turn red before stepping into the flow of traffic. Once the traffic light changed to red, he walked over to the first car; he showed the driver Nate's picture.

"Have you seen this boy at any time today?" Joyce asked, making sure he had a gentle smile on his face. All the occupants, two men in their early twenties and three girls, right out of high school, shook their heads no. Joyce pulled the picture back and tapped on the roof of the car, saying, "Thanks, have a safe night." He looked at the car directly behind and signaled for the driver to slow down. The woman driver in her late forties immediately slowed down and stopped next to Joyce. "Did I do something wrong, Officer?"

Joyce smiled and said, "No, ma'am, just seeking the public's help in finding this missing boy."

He showed Nate's picture to the woman. "Sorry, I haven't seen him. I'm not from this area. My daughter is entering NYU in September. I would like you to meet her," the woman said.

"I'm usually over in the Village on McDougal Street, Tuesdays through Saturday," Joyce said innocently.

A female officer walked over to Joyce and tugged on his uniform shirt. "Bob, I heard what you said to that woman, you're married," Officer Carol Bini commented.

"I know that, but if I blow her off here, Harry, Pat, and Big Mike will never have a chance to meet someone. There are disadvantages of being a foot cop with these bullshit hours. How is a guy or a girl ever going to meet someone halfway decent?" The light was about to turn red. "Let's ask a few more drivers if they have seen the kid," Joyce said.

"Bobby, these cars are either from Westchester, Long Island, or New Jersey. The neighborhood residents, who live in this area, are in their houses," Bini said. She stood five feet nine inches tall, brown eyes, she wore red lipstick and had an endearing smile which she used on the younger male drivers.

The first two cars stopped for her and offered her no help, but she did get their telephone numbers for what they thought was a relationship but she simply wrote down the number next to the driver's name and submitted it.

"I know doing this is a jerk job, but it looks good. The sergeant likes proactive work from his cops," she said.

"Officer Joyce, I need to speak to you for a minute," Sergeant Gregory shouted. Joyce and Bini walked over to the sergeant.

"Officer Bini, you can go back to questioning the motorists, I just need Joyce." Bini turned and Joyce handed her his copy of Nate's photograph. Sergeant Gregory waited until Bini was out of earshot.

"Hey, Bobby, sorry I didn't pick you to shadow the detectives. I wanted you to do a one-man search of the little boy's building."

"Thanks, boss, but I have no idea where the little boy's building is located," Joyce said. Bob Piccione stood five feet eight inches tall with arms of a weightlifter and the personality of a truck driver. Sergeant Gregory preferred him to be his driver as he could have control over the hot-headed Italian. Pic, as the sergeant called him, enjoyed the comfort of the patrol car's air conditioning in the hot summer and the heat on the cold winter nights.

"Pic, I'll need you to show Joyce the boy's building. I want you back here immediately to take down all the names and assignment changes during our stay tonight," Sergeant Gregory said as Pic and Joyce walked north on West Broadway to Nate's apartment building.

Prince Street Building
2230 Hours

The freight elevator was noisy, dirty, and unsafe, but the building manager requested that all uniformed police officers use it to keep the residents unaware of their presence in the building. Joyce used his night stick to keep the elevator doors from closing completely and returning to the ground floor, he got out of the elevator on the top floor. His memo book kept the roof door from locking behind him as he walked out onto the roof. The first thing he did as the door hit his memo book was to jump up and grab the roof edge of the stairwell shed. He pulled himself up and over the top, allowing one hand to hold his body up as he grabbed his flashlight and scanned the roof—nothing. He quietly lowered himself down. His division radio had been turned down low by order of Sergeant Jaffee. He was now alone on the building's edge, straddling the two-foot-high wall surrounding the building's roof. It was an unusually warm night and many of the apartments had all their windows completely opened. He was disgusted when he saw the man in bikini briefs get up from the couch, holding the hand of a very underage boy. He remembered the roll call instructions about the sensitivity to the residents of the Village and SoHo and surrounding communities. This was the height of the NAMBLA rising, the abbreviation meant National Association of Man-Boy Love Affair. The politicians in the Village, SoHo, and others were very sensitive about the police interfering in the so-called rights of these individuals. Joyce saw the man walk over to his apartment door and open it. There stood another man in similar bikini briefs smiling. The man in the hallway had a handful of money which he gave to the man with the boy. The little boy didn't hesitate; he simply went with the other man. Joyce wanted to vomit. He kicked off the wall and turned away. Joyce to himself, *This is one messed-up neighborhood and they let their son walk through this shit this morning, alone. I'm not certain that I can believe them.*

Joyce continued with his search. He picked up his memo book and let the roof door close and lock behind him as he walked to the elevator and removed his night stick. He checked the stairway closest to him, there was no one. He walked along the hallway to the far side stairway and checked the stairs up to the roof door and checked the top of it before returning to the stairs. He walked down the flight of stairs and checked the next stairway landing—nothing. He walked across the hallway to the original stairway, he rechecked up the stairway with his flashlight, then walked down to the next floor.

The floors to the building were made for factory use and were much higher and wider than residential ones. The stairs went down ten steps, there was a small landing then another ten steps to the next floor below. He repeated this search process. Suddenly there was a robbery in progress in the Thirteenth Precinct on Third Avenue. He turned his radio up louder to listen. He stepped out of the stairway to do a hallway check when he saw the uniformed officer sitting in a chair and a man in a suit talking with a woman. He lowered the volume on his radio and continued to walk toward the officer, still listening to the robbery in progress. Joyce turned up the volume as he neared the woman and the detective. Joyce recognized the detective from a previous arrest he made in the First

Precinct. The robbery call was unfounded, Joyce turned down the volume to his radio.

The officer sitting on the chair signaled for Joyce to bend down. He handed Joyce a copy of the boy's picture. "She's the boy's mother and the guy inside is the father," he whispered. Joyce looked at them both, the mother never acknowledged him, neither did the father. Joyce continued his stairwell search until he entered the basement. He pulled out his set of lock picks and went to work. He had all the doors unlocked in the basement in ten minutes. Once opened, he closed and relocked them. He wanted to make sure whoever was inside didn't come out while he was searching another room. Twelve pieces of paper were needed to complete this, but Joyce had been prepared. He folded each piece of paper until the paper fit snugly between the doorjamb and the door itself. If someone were to open the door, chances are they would not notice the small piece of paper which would have fallen to the floor. He completed his search but did not find the boy or his remains. He was satisfied that he had completed the task the sergeant had entrusted him with.

An Hour Later

Joyce walked back to the van, which was now the THV or the "Temporary Headquarters Vehicle." The van would be the meeting point where everyone assigned to the case would report to and have their rank, name, shield number, and time of arrival logged into a book. Sergeant Gregory had Pic log in all the NSU II cops, the First Precinct detectives, and the original cops who were assigned to the job, as he waited for the duty captain. Joyce walked over to Sergeant Gregory, he hated Sergeant Jaffee. He believed she should never have been assigned as a training sergeant. She loved her women and hated men, but that was as far as Joyce wanted to go with it.

"Hey, Sarge, I did a rooftop to basement search, nothing. I mean I checked the top of the stairway enclosure on the roof, the way we were taught, and all the way to the basement. I opened every door in the basement."

"Hey, wait just a minute, you opened every door in the basement?"

"Yup, remember Veronica, the tall redhead, my old foot partner. Well she and her husband were locksmiths and she taught me a bunch of stuff. 'I could unlock the gate to the stairway to heaven,' as she often said."

Sergeant Gregory shook his head at Joyce's innocence. "Bobby, did you check for a backpack, I forgot to tell you about that," Sergeant Gregory said.

"Boss, I checked for everything, I found nothing, nada."

"Bobby, you seem a little, you know, like a little depressed and you are never depressed."

"It's nuttin'."

"Bobby, we have been working as a team for a while, and you . . . and don't ever repeat this to no one . . . are one of the best cops I have ever worked with in my career."

"Okay, look, my daughter is teething and I have to take care of her when I get home. It gives my wife a few hours of sleep. I love my daughter and after tonight I will hold my daughter so tightly, she may scream, but I . . . well . . . this area . . . is messed up."

Suddenly a man appeared, Joyce recognized him as the man in the apartment, the missing boy's father.

"Hey, guys . . . and ladies, I have made some more pictures of my son, Nate. If you could show them around to the people passing by, maybe someone saw him walking alone this morning."

Joyce walked over to the man and extended his hand. "I'll take one and start showing it to the people in the cars passing by."

Alan Zapata looked at Joyce then turned away but immediately turned around and handed a picture to him. "Thank you, Officer, for trying to find my son." Joyce looked down at the picture and then at the man's hand. It was dirty with very obvious dirt under his unusually long fingernails.

Joyce walked over to the curb and wanted to rip the picture into little pieces but instead turned on his "Happy ta meet ya" face. Joyce to himself, *Carol is right, the people in these cars are not from this neighborhood. They are here from out of town for a few drinks and maybe get lucky. They're not the locals who would have been on the street this morning. He is trying to lead us somewhere, anywhere, just as long as it is away from the boy . . . or his body.*

Sergeant Gregory saw Joyce getting upset and walked over to him. "Bobby, go EOT in the van and that's an order."

Later That Night

The remainder of the unit returned to the van. Joyce sat up with his back against the back wall of the van, he didn't say a word. The van was dark except for the light coming from the overhead street lamp. *What the hell was the father doing if he spends his day developing pictures? He couldn't walk his son to the bus stop,* Joyce thought.

Sergeant Gregory had convinced the bodega owner to allow him to conduct a quick roll call for his officers. The cops stood in two lines.

Officer Carol Bini was the first to speak. "Hey, Joyce, you've been a little quiet tonight."

"For Joyce, that's a major improvement," a voice said from the back. The officers laughed, they were tired.

"I was just thinking about this little boy," Joyce said as he stood in formation. Bini moved up and stood next to him.

"Bobby, we did our job and searched the area for the little guy tonight. Now it's in the detectives' hands," she whispered. "Yeah, I guess so."

Bini turned and looked at Joyce. "Bobby, you never give up, so why now give in?" she said.

"You got kids?" he asked.

"Two, a girl six and my son is two, why do you ask?"

Joyce put his cap on his head and turned to her. "How would you react if one of them went missing, but you're not a cop, just a civilian, talking to a detective in the hallway of your building? Suddenly a cop in uniform comes through the stairwell door and approaches you and the detective. Would you stop your conversation and ask the cop if he had any news?"

"Absolutely, and if the cop didn't, I'd be pissed," she replied.

"When I did my vertical of the building, as the Sarge ordered, I came out of the stairwell onto the victim's floor and a woman was talking with a detective. It was a very soft conversation, the detective turned to me as did the uniformed cop who was sitting on a chair in the hallway. The boy's mother never turned to me, no questions, no hi, hey, nothing."

Joyce stood with the other officers of NSU II as the sergeant checked each officer's activity for the evening. He looked up from the paperwork, then checked his roll call. Everyone was accounted for.

"Listen up. We may be back here tomorrow to continue the search. Know what you searched and where it was."

Joyce stepped out of formation and walked over to the two large refrigerators which held beer and soda and looked behind it and then pulled himself to the top and checked. He lowered himself and brushed off his hand and fell back into formation.

"All right, everyone into the van, it's EOT," Gregory said. No one said a word, the boy was still missing. Nothing was said as the officers slowly made their way into the boxed prisoner van. Joyce made his way to the back and sat with his back to the rear wall.

"Hey, Bobby, what did you expect to find behind the refrigerator?" a voice said from the darkness.

"I guess I was hoping to find something, anything, a clue, but all I got was nothing," Joyce said.

Joyce closed his eyes and wanted to sleep, but all he could envision was the little boy's face from the pictures he now had one in his memo book and one in his uniformed hat.

Thirteenth Precinct
End of Tour

The prisoner van stopped in the middle of Twenty-First Street, directly in front of the station house door. The officers hurried off the van and walked quickly into the station house then ran up the stairs to their locker room. Bini grabbed and held Joyce's hand until they were the only two in the van besides Pic.

"Let's go, last stop, all off," Pic said jokingly. Joyce and Bini stepped off as Pic gunned the engine.

"Can we have a drink and discuss this, but not in a precinct spot," Bini asked. Joyce took a step back.

"I could go for beer, but where?" Joyce asked.

"Pete's Tavern, it's on Irving Place," she said.

"They charge, we pay for our own," Joyce said coldly.

"Absolutely," she said with a smile.

Joyce rushed into the locker room and took off his uniform and ran into the shower. A voice from the back of the locker room shouted, "Bobby's got a date."

"No, I don't," Joyce shouted over the noise of the shower.

Three other anonymous officers sang in unison, "Bobby's got a date and he ain't telling."

Pete's Tavern

Joyce pulled his car up to the crosswalk and waited until Carol parked her car behind his before he opened his driver's side door. He slid his precinct parking permit onto his dashboard and stepped out and looked around for the DOT parking signs. No Standing Any Time was the wording on the red sign. *Perfect*, he thought to himself. He gently took Carol's hand and they kissed. "I needed that," they said simultaneously and laughed. They walked the block to Pete's Tavern holding hands. They stopped at the aging tavern door and hugged. You smell good. Took a shower? Like we were going on a date. Joyce wrapped both his arms around Carol Bini and smiled.

"Sorry, I don't date cops, besides I am married with a nine-month-old daughter who already has dibs on my heart."

"Then, let's have a drink for Nate. The boy's name was Nate, right?" she asked.

Joyce didn't say a word, he stepped ahead of Bini and opened the front door to the tavern. Suddenly the bartender called out, "Last call."

The bartender walked over to the couple. "I'm having a two-for-one sale. Once I close the register, I come around and sit with my friends."

Joyce looked at the large stomach of the bartender. "Thank you, Jim, but this is a private, personal conversation, nothing against you, but we need the time. Next time you can sit with us," Joyce explained.

The door opened and a gorgeous blonde entered and smiled at the bartender. Joyce smiled and wanted to pat the bartender on his thick shoulder.

Carol adjusted her chair to get closer to Joyce. "So you've been here before."

"My wife and I met here. Jimmy, the bartender, married us that night. He was my 'best' man at the 'wedding.'"

"Sorry, I wanted to go to a safe place. I didn't know you were here before," Carol said. She wanted to hold Joyce close but sat back in her captain's chair with a bar-stool bottom.

"Bobby, if you were not married, I would dump my husband and beg you to marry me." Joyce looked over to see the bartender sitting next to the blonde.

"Carol, can we talk?" he asked. They talked until they finished their two beers. They could tell the bartender wanted them to leave. They walked and talked but every conversation seemed to return to the missing boy. She stopped at Joyce's car and turned to him.

"Gerry is taking me on a 'second honeymoon' next week. Tomorrow will be our last tour until I come back."

"How long is this vacation and why am I only hearing about it now?" he said.

"Gerry was able to switch his vacation pick with another fireman. His parents have a house on Virginia Beach and they will not be using it. They even made me an offer I couldn't refuse. They are going to babysit my kids while we are away. I guess I'll come back pregnant again. So please, don't call out tomorrow."

Later That Morning
Joyce's House

Joyce sat on the floor with his legs folded and a blanket in the open space. He was asleep with his arms holding his daughter while still fully clothed. Elizabeth stood at the doorway with her arms crossed as she leaned against the doorjamb. She had been watching her husband and their daughter for the last twenty minutes.

"Bob, it's time for me to feed Jennifer," she said softly as Jennifer began to wiggle. "Bob, are you awake?"

"I am now, but just give me a few more minutes with her."

"Bad night last night?"

"Oh yeah. If I were not a cop, I would never believe that so much crap could go on in one freaken' neighborhood."

"Bob, give me Jenn, she'll be awake in two minutes. This way you can do your ten miles and we can have breakfast together."

Joyce picked up his still-sleeping daughter and handed her to his wife. He unfolded his legs and stood up unassisted. He began his stretching exercises as Elizabeth held their daughter. A few minutes later, he slammed the front door. That awakened Jenn, who went into a full-out cry. Elizabeth unfastened her top and allowed Jenn to begin feeding. Ten minutes later, Elizabeth heard a loud thunder clap. Suddenly the rain poured down, Jenn was finished and Elizabeth put her in her bassinet, while she set up towels for her husband's return.

6

The Detectives' Turn

First Police Precinct
0645 Hours

Sergeant Harvey Fuchs, a forty-six-year-old bachelor and a thirty-four-year-veteran of the NYPD, was the commander of the detective night watch for the previous ten years. He was a cross between Columbo and Alan Alda. Some detectives would say he could come at you from four sides simultaneously. He was aggressive but understanding, at times. His personal van was his second home. It contained all the equipment he and his detectives needed at any given time. Though never married, he always had a woman barely over the age of twenty-one on his arm at any police social event. He stood five feet eleven inches tall and never broke one fifty on the scale, his soft green eyes and long black hair were what made him stand out in a crowd. He stepped out of the squad commander's office and walked into the middle of the open area between the green metal desks.

"Hey, guys, and of course, ladies, I want your honest opinions, on this one. Ed, you go first."

Ed Polise, nine-year veteran, third year working night watch. "Sarge, the parents at the bus stop need to be interviewed. If they confirm that the kid got on the bus with their own kids, we go after the bus driver or the janitor. Those parents are key to this."

"Ron," Fuchs said.

Ron Jewett, an eleven-year veteran, his seventh year with night watch. "The squad will need to interview the NSU cops who responded. I know they were not the initial responding unit, but they were there long after the day tour left. They did a better job of searching the buildings."

"Al."

Al Ronaldson's first day on night watch. "I get the idea that photos were needed, but it was a Friday evening and the only people on the streets were people who wanted to party."

"Jack."

Jack Ronaldson, no relationship to Al, was a fifteen-year detective veteran, in his last year of policing. "They, the people in their cars, didn't give a crap about the kid. That woman was one cool broad. Down the road, she and her husband will have to take a lie detector test," Ronaldson said.

Sergeant Fuchs had been sitting on the small railing that divided the waiting room from the detectives' work area. He made notes in his small memo pad. He stood up and took a small breath.

"Remember none of this leaves this office. I will tell you this, I have a friend, a retired lieutenant who hires himself to test people. He told me straight out he couldn't prove when a person was lying. There was no solid evidence. He was adamant when he said to me, 'If you brought in and asked a perp to take a polygraph test voluntarily, he the tester could never testify to the results, even if he believed the suspect was lying.' It's a game. You ask questions, and after the person has answered the questions, you say the machine says you are lying. Some people collapse and admit their guilt and others stay strong and challenge the results. According to my lieutenant friend, there is nothing you can use to prove the guilt or innocence of a suspect taking a lie detector test."

"That would freaken' suck, if it ever got out," Al Ronaldson said.

"That's why what happens in this room stays in this room. Now let's get back to our own office and sign out. All fives go in this envelope," Fuchs said as he held up a yellow departmental multiuse envelope.

"I'll have the desk safeguard it until the sergeant comes in."

"I'm here," Sergeant Lawrence said as he walked straight to his office.

"The cavalry is here, now we can go home," Fuchs said as he handed off the multiuse envelope to the squad commander.

Later

Lawrence sat at his desk and read over the night watch's DD5s or simply fives. The team, from last evening, was scheduled to do their day tour, which gave the case a little more continuity.

"Hey, Vin, I want you to go to the kid's school and interview the principal, then go to the school bus garage and find out the name of the driver and go to his house and interview him."

"The guys went to interview the school bus driver, but his wife said he was away for the weekend. Then her boyfriend arrived to retrieve his sport jacket which he forgot. It was a little embarrassing for her, the guys had a good laugh afterwards," Carlson said.

"Got it, boss, but it is Saturday, in the middle of the Memorial Day weekend. Do you expect the principal to be at the school on a holiday weekend?" Carlson asked.

"He will today, I reached out to him this morning. He begrudgingly agreed, but he wants to be on Long Island for an afternoon barbecue," Lawrence said.

"Got it, boss, I'll take Frank with me, he speaks the language," Carlson said.

The sergeant's phone rang. "Hey, Tony, what's up that I get a call so early in the morning from the borough?"

Officer Tony White was a thirty-year veteran, spending the last twenty years in the office of the borough commander.

"Sarge, the freaken' kid's story is all over the media. The chief wants you to give a briefing on the search here at eleven sharp. Look good, boss, he's gonna let you do the talking on this one." Lawrence looked at Vin who grabbed his suit jacket from behind his chair and raced out the door. *I got shit on this, and the borough wants me to give a presentation at eleven, then have me face the media. I'm not the freaken' DCPI. Let me do what I do, find the bad guys. I don't need to do no dancing in front of the cameras,* he thought.

"Tell the chief I'll be there," Lawrence said and put the receiver into its cradle.

All the detectives were looking at their boss. "Good, now that I've got your attention, how about you guys get me some information to feed to the hungry lions."

Carlson reentered the squad room, "Hey, Sarge, I'm gonna head to the bus garage first and chat with the driver's boss. Then I'll go to the driver's house. He will be a little more receptive to me if I have his boss's approval. I'll chat with the principal afterward, he's not going anywhere until after I interview him."

"That works," Lawrence said and turned to the two remaining detectives in the squad room as he looked at his wristwatch.

"Hey, Tommy and Joey, how about you guys go to the bus stop on Tuesday morning. Chat up the parents, or any adults standing with a little one. Then go to the school and check with their list of who should have been at what bus stop with their kids yesterday morning."

"On it, boss," Joey said.

"Say while you are at the bus stop, interview the bodega workers, you might get lucky," Lawrence said and checked them off the list to be interviewed. "I'll put the two of you out of service for the first four hours," Lawrence continued.

Patrol Borough Manhattan South
1100 Hours

Lawrence sat at the large conference room table, normally used for witness or prisoner interviews. He glanced down at his notes and wondered what stupid questions the press would ask him at this meeting. He looked at the podium, there were only three microphones with identifiers attached to the wooden podium. *The media response was minimal at best*, he thought. Only a few local stations had responded to the NYPD's request for a press conference.

The seats at the oval oak table were occupied by the two-star borough commander and his assistant, a one star, who was seated to the left of the two star. The division inspectors with their assistants, the oak leaf deputy inspectors, occupied the remaining seats at the table. The precinct commanders and their squad commanders occupied the outlying chairs, usually metal folding ones. Sergeant

Lawrence stood up and walked to the podium and began, "Chief, I will give you everything we have on the Nate Zapata case, the Little Boy from SoHo, who went missing yesterday."

Chief Pragmethius, a thirty-year veteran, son of Greek immigrants, spent his last twenty-four years as a leader. He had a chiseled jaw, large forehead, salt and pepper hair, square shoulders, deep-set eyes, large hands. The chief always liked his supervisors to stand at a podium to give presentation or hold a press conference dressed as though they were going to their own funeral. If you came unprepared, he would not hesitate to embarrass you, no matter the level of your rank. "Proceed, Sergeant, I didn't mean to put you on the spot, but for the sake of information for all, Lieutenant Fenty is out sick and is not expected to return any time soon. That is closed for discussion."

Sergeant Lawrence stood squarely behind the podium, he had placed his notes on its thirty-degree angled top. He had memorized all the information and reminded himself to look down occasionally, just to appear a little unprepared.

He began, “Nate Zapata went missing on Friday, May 25, at about eighteen hundred hours.”

Pragmethius interrupted, “Sarge, I thought the child went missing in the morning.”

“Chief, there was a call received by the First Precinct’s switchboard operator at eighteen hundred hours yesterday. A woman identified herself as Arlene Zapata, living at 227 Spring Street. She stated her son had taken his school bus for the first time in the morning and for some reason he never arrived home.”

Pragmethius immediately stood up and walked to the podium. “Thank you all for coming,” he said and nodded to Lawrence. “That is all the information we have for now. We will call you for another press conference when we have any new information for the public,” he said. Pragmethius waited as the angry reporters unfastened their microphones from the top of the podium. He stood firmly holding the top of the podium. He grew testy as he waited for the reporters to pack up their equipment and be escorted out of the Borough Headquarters. Pragmethius walked back and sat down in his chair after the last reporter walked out the door as the precinct cop closed and locked it. Lawrence returned to the podium and looked at the Chief.

“Continue Sergeant.”

“We did a preliminary search of the boy’s building and the immediate surrounding area, with negative results. We did a canvass of the buildings in the vicinity, and NSU I is currently searching the empty lots by the World Trade Center. We have interviewed the boy's parents separately and their stories match."

"Why did they wait so long to notify the police department that their son went missing?" Pragmethius asked.

"The mother said she allowed her son to take the school bus for the first time, alone, that morning. The mother further stated she never told her cousin that she allowed her son to take his school bus alone that morning, and that he was allowed to return home on the bus after school, because she, her cousin, didn't have a telephone where she lived. She stated her cousin Sophie usually met her son after school at the bus stop on Friday afternoons. She would take him for a walk, so he wouldn't interrupt his mother's day-care sessions. She thought Sophie picked up her son as she always did and took him for their usual walk. When it went past seventeen hundred hours, she decided to call some of the other mothers at the bus stop. They told her that her son never arrived at the bus stop that morning. That is when she called the police."

Chief Pragmethius sat up straight in his chair as the others followed. "That is not to be given to the press. I want this story to be one of a little boy who got lost around his school."

Sergeant Lawrence looked down at his notes. "Er, Chief, could we have a moment in your office?"

Interior Chief Pragmethius's Office

The chief slipped behind his desk and sat in his personal large black leather chair as Sergeant Lawrence stood behind the only folding metal chair in the room.

"Sir, I believe the boy never got on the school bus that morning. I have my detectives interviewing the bus driver as we speak. They will also try to interview the parents of the other children, who normally took the school bus along with the Zapata boy. That may take a few days since this is a holiday weekend."

"Very good, Sergeant."

"I have ordered my detectives to find this supposed cousin 'Sophie' and bring her in for questioning. If there is really a Sophie. I will have my detectives do a background check on this woman. They have also been ordered to get the landlord to give them a list of all the tenants in the Zapatas' building. They will wait for the mailman and interview him. They are to go through every piece of mail addressed to their building. I want them to record the name on each envelope and also record the accompanying name on the return address label. When the background checks have been completed of the residents of the Zapatas' building, we will look into the names of the return address label. We will do this for two consecutive weeks."

"Sergeant, when you get promoted to lieutenant, I want you to give me a call. Now let's get back to the meeting and give the others nothing. I will have to brief the commissioner himself."

"The commissioner, sir," Lawrence said.

"Yes, SoHo and the lower Manhattan area around the World Trade Center are transitioning, and the property owners, as well as the real estate board, have a very keen interest in the redevelopment of SoHo and the financial district. We have to be very careful as to what is said to the press. Nothing comes from you without my approval. You funnel everything through me directly. Anything that gets to the press and can be linked back to you will be a career ender for you. Do you understand, Sergeant?"

"Yes, sir," Lawrence said meekly.

"Now let's get back to the meeting. It will end very quickly. I have a meeting with the mayor's people after I meet with the commissioner."

"Yes, sir, I understand."

7

Have Another Look

Thirteenth Police Precinct
Saturday May 26th
1730 Hours

Sergeant Gregory sat at the table and looked over the limited roll call. He would be the only supervisor for the night's patrol. Bobby Joyce walked by and stopped. "Hey, Sarge, any news on the little guy we were looking for last night? Did he finally show up at home?" Joyce asked quickly.

"Sorry, Bobby, but they have nothing to report, it looks as if the little guy just disappeared off the street. I will be handling out additional photos for the troops at roll call. Now go suit up, we have roll call in fifteen minutes."

Roll Call

Sergeant Gregory pulled the large room partitions so that the room was now half its size. He needed the privacy for his NSU II officers. It allowed him to conduct his roll call and give the officers any information they needed for their night's patrol. It would also be away from the prying eyes of the public, if they should enter the station house.

Twelve members of the unit were now seated in the school-style desks. The desks never worked for Joyce. His .38 revolver hung on his right hip though he was primarily left handed. His left arm was never supported by the desk extension as it did for right-handed people.

"Attention roll call, this conversation is strictly among members of the department. The Detectives and the powers that be believe the little boy never made it to school yesterday morning. His mother said she allowed him to go to school alone yesterday for the first time. She told the detectives she did watch him go all the way to the bus stop. She said her son got on the bus and it left," Gregory said.

Joyce got a sting in his right anklebone, it was a quick kick from Bini. He ignored it for the moment.

"Hey, Sarge, are we gonna search for the little guy tonight?" Joyce asked.

"No, they had NSU 1 out in the pouring rain all day. They spent the entire tour searching through those empty lots downtown by the World Trade Center."

"That's quite a distance from the kid's home," an unidentified officer said.

"They started searching from the apartment and made their way all the way downtown to Chambers Street in the pouring rain. They were let go early, they were completely soaked," Gregory said.

"Dismissed, back to command, no meal," Joyce said. Everyone laughed softly.

"Something like that," Gregory said without looking up from his roll call.

"Only the best for the NYPD," Joyce murmured.

"We just relay the messages that come down from the palace. If it was up to me, I would have everyone prepared for a long night's search, but it's not. Take your rain gear with you, just in case. Listen up on your radios, we still could get mobilized to search for the kid. Remember if we do get mobilized, expect a ton of reporters following your every move. You will have to go through the motions for them. "Say nothing, and for God's sake, act like professionals out there. You have your assignments and meals, now pick up your radios and take your posts."

Joyce and Bini approached Sergeant Gregory. "Hey, Sarge, Carol and I have adjoining posts tonight. Would it be all right if we worked together? She needs some movers and I doubt if you would want her to do car stops alone."

Gregory scanned the roll call and the officer's activity sheets for the month. "Joyce, you take a twenty-two-hundred meal. Bini, you take a twenty-three-hundred meal. I want to see your activity before you sign out."

Joyce gave Gregory a half salute. "Ten-four, Sarge." Joyce walked quickly to get Bini's attention; he tapped her arm as she was about to step into the old box van. "Hey, step out for a second."

Bini turned and walked with Joyce. "How did you know I was down for the month?" she said.

"Sarge keeps a running tally of all our activity, and I got a look. Your activity was highlighted in red and so was your monthly total of one mover."

"Yeah, and what was yours highlighted in . . . gold stars," she said.

"It keeps me from thinking about my daughter, and now with this Zapata kid missing, I need to be occupied," Joyce said.

Sergeant Gregory interrupted their conversation. "Joyce, Bini, I need you both inside the building . . . *now*," Gregory said loudly.

"Oh shit, they're in trouble," an anonymous officer groaned.

Thirteenth Precinct, Sergeant's Locker Room

Sergeant Gregory walked the two officers to the solitude of the sergeant's locker room, neither Joyce nor Bini had ever been in or seen the inside of a sergeant's locker room. Gregory took a quick check of the interior. He signaled for the two officers to enter. He closed and locked the door, put his clipboard on the table, and looked at the two officers. It was a small cluttered room with a long table in the middle of the room with four folding chairs, one on each side. A small couch and refrigerator were on the far wall.

"I checked with the borough and got clearance so that the two of you could continue to search for the little boy, but only after Bini gets her activity up to par."

"Sorry, Sarge," she said.

"I want to see activity and lots of it. If a car takes a light, do an inspection on the car and the driver, that always helped me when I was low," Gregory said. Then he relaxed his body and put his arms over the roll call sheets.

"The borough gave me a car for the two of you to use. Smash it up and the two of you will be walking for the remainder of your careers."

Gregory tossed the car keys to Joyce, who lobbed them over to Bini. "Carol, you take the first half, and I'll take the second half. Oh, Sarge, do you still want us to stagger our meals?" Joyce asked.

"No, take a twenty-three-hundred meal, and I do not want to see the two of you in here on meal. Take it in the RMP. Like we used to in the old days," Gregory said and smiled.

"Any reason I get to drive the first half?" Bini asked as they walked out of the station house and began looking for their patrol car.

"Yeah, I drive my wife everywhere, it's about time I got driven around."

"Bob, if I hadn't met your wife, I would have thrown these back in your face. I will do it for Liz."

Later in SoHo

Joyce and Bini sat in their new patrol car at the curb across the street and a hundred feet east of the entrance to the Zapatas' apartment house. They talked about the car stop they made twenty seconds into their tour. *Bini had walked over to Joyce's side and unlocked his door and opened it for him. He was actually embarrassed by it, but didn't say a word. She drove to the corner and waited for the red light to change, and as it did, a car flew through the intersection. Bini drove into the intersection and positioned her car behind the offending vehicle. They could see the reverse white lights quickly flash on then off, an indication the car's driver had put his car in park. Joyce and Bini timed their exits perfectly. It was as though they had been radio car partners for years. The driver came out of his car, dressed in satin dress pants and a white sleeveless T-shirt. Joyce always referred to them as something Bini considered an ethnic slur. The driver's hair was slicked back. The driver's hands were all over the place as he went through the litany of cops and people he knew. Bini was cool, but Joyce walked around the car to stand next to his partner.*

"Hey, do yoose guys know who my fadder is, do ya know who he is?" It was Joyce's turn. Joyce grabbed the man by his greasy hair and threw him against his car and slammed his face onto the windshield. Joyce put his greasy hand over the man's mouth. What Joyce whispered to the man almost made her pee her uniform pants. "Look, pal, if you don't know who your father is, how the hell am I supposed to know?" The man's body went limp.

Seven moving summonses later, Carol was out of the red and into the black for her summonses. Now they could search for the little boy for the remainder of the tour.

"I love the smell of a new car. Growing up we never had a new car, always a secondhand car. My dad worked as a parks department supervisor and he always smelled of cut grass, no matter what time of year it was," Bini said absently.

"My dad worked for the housing authority as a buyer. We too had several used cars. They were always breaking down on my dad. He'd spend his entire Saturday working to fix the problem with the car, only to have it break down on us when we were headed to church that following Sunday morning. In fact, his first new car was a station wagon to fit all us six kids. I don't know how we, six kids, four boys and two girls, and both parents, survived growing up in Brooklyn in a brownstone house that was built in 1915 with only *one* bathroom," Joyce said.

"You lived in a brownstone?" Bini asked.

"Well, it wasn't exactly a brownstone like the ones in Downtown Brooklyn or Uptown Manhattan. They were sort of attached four-bedroom houses," he said.

"Four bedrooms, that's a mansion."

"Two bedrooms were small single-rooms, the others were large rooms. One for my parents and one for the three of us younger boys. My older brother and sister occupied the two small rooms. My baby sister grew up in a crib until my oldest brother went into the army, she got his room. The three of us boys still had to share the same room."

"Did you take care of your younger sister?"

"Took her to and from school every day."

"Would you let anything happen to her?"

"Do I look like I would let anything happen to my baby sister?"

"This conversation is over, now what?" she said.

Joyce got out of the car, Bini followed. He stood at the entrance to the former factory building and looked west to West Broadway.

"His mother said she followed her son to the bus stop which was a block and a half away."

Joyce pointed in the direction of the bus stop. "It's down there," Joyce said.

"Yeah, so what?" Bini asked. Joyce walked to the school bus stop, she followed.

"The signs, nothing but three-hour commercial vehicle standing only allowed. She could have followed him, but there were no trees for her to hide behind, you know, in case he turned around. If she went across the street to have the trucks hide her from his view, she wouldn't be able to keep him in her line of sight. Remember, this was a yellow school bus stop, so there were no painted yellow curbs for school buses. Trucks could have been in the spot, which forced the children to walk between the parked trucks to get onto their school bus. If that was the case, there was no way his mother could have seen him get onto his school bus except for her being right next to him at the school bus stop," Joyce said.

"How do you know that trucks were parked along this street that early in the morning?" she asked.

"We're doing ten by sixes next week. We'll meet here at seven in the morning on our next set of day tours, and if I am right, you're buying breakfast," Joyce said.

"Okay, but I can't do it with you next week, I'll be away, remember? So the trucks blocked her view. I'll accept that," she said.

"Tell me how did she see him get on his bus. I will need to talk with the detectives on that point. Let's go to lower Manhattan, where the NSU I guys had to do their search," Joyce said.

In the Shadow of the World Trade Center

Joyce and Bini leaned against the fender of their patrol car and stared at the lights of the World Trade Center.

"I timed our run from the Zapata's building to the entrance of the Holland Tunnel, it was fifteen seconds, and we weren't speeding, just routine patrol," Joyce said.

"Seven or eight seconds for a car that was speeding but not so fast as to draw attention," Bini remarked.

"By the time someone found a public telephone that worked, the car would be already on I-78," Joyce said.

"Exactly."

"It's an option for the detectives."

"So why are we down here, you don't seem to care about that option," she said.

"I do consider it, but there is more to this picture. Carol, those twin towers are the symbol of what we are, what America is. This flat land, from where we stand to those towers stand, was the heart of early New York a long time ago. The early industries started here, sewing, plumbing, and hardware supplies. This was the hub of the industrial revolution. Now it is razed ground. The city didn't condemn those two- and three-story buildings to make ball fields, they wanted to make this a residential community," Joyce said.

"You've got to be kidding me."

"Not according to a friend of mine. The overall plan will have schools, residential apartment houses, out in the open waters of the Hudson, and here on dry land. This entire area will be totally unrecognizable in ten to fifteen years."

“Bob, that is scary, that you know all of that information.”

“Carol, I was at a first precinct community council meeting three months ago and there was only one guy present. He was the only resident in the community from Chambers Street to the Battery from Broadway to the water. They want people here, rich people, and that won’t happen if this case isn’t resolved quickly.”

“You can’t mean that all this property will be not be sold over one little boy’s disappearance.”

“No, but if it ever got out that there are hundreds of NAMBLA men living in SoHo, in the shadows of this area, development may not go as quickly as anticipated.”

“Do you think one of those pervs took the little boy for themselves?”

“No, but if it is suggested to the press, and the right journalist or a news reporter puts together a good story, this property will be a ghost town for another thirty years,” he said.

“That would put a crimp in their plans.”

“A major crimp and I wouldn’t want to be the cop who put the crimp there. That would be a career ender. He or she would be buried out in Staten Island for the remainder of their days, even if they were promoted,” Joyce said.

“Hey, Bobby, how about we set up a meeting with these people and put out what we know, maybe they would give us a couple of houses to keep us quiet,” she said jokingly.

“Just to let you know, and this goes no further. Whenever I am home and my telephone rings just once, I pick up the receiver. There is dead air, then I get the dial tone. I asked Elizabeth if that has happened to her and she said no. I'm being watched, for whatever reason."

Carol tilted her head and semi-smiled at Joyce.

"Carol, they don't joke around. We would be residents *in* the Staten Island landfill in a matter of days."

"I'm gonna need a drink after this, at Pete's, but only you and I," she said.

8

The Usual Suspects
First Precinct Squad Room

Sergeant Lawrence sat in his office, as he read the DD5s from the day tour. In walked Detective Carlson who pretended to knock on his boss's office door.

"Hey, Sarge, any of the usual, compulsive confessors come in to surrender today. You know, for taking the boy," Carlson asked jokingly.

"It looks like the media has decided to hold on to the story until after the holiday weekend. My telephone has been quiet all morning," Lawrence said.

"Maybe the puzzle palace wants to give us a chance to do our job and solve this case for a change," Carlson said.

"Yeah, like that would ever happen."

"Well, they're holding on to the info, for whatever reason," Carlson said.

"You're a first grade, I want you to stay with this investigation until we solve it, one way or another," Lawrence quipped.

"My new girlfriend is going to be very happy, that I'll be doing steady days for a while."

Sergeant Lawrence held out a DD5 for his detective.

"I was looking over your five from the first night, it looks as though you changed what the mother initially said."

"Yeah, well, she told me that she watched her son from the apartment window and I put that in my notes. Then her husband came and they walked off briefly to discuss something, and when she returned, she stated that she actually went with her son to the street and watched him from the door."

"You didn't question her about what she told you earlier?" Lawrence said.

"Her husband was listening to every word she said. I tried to close the apartment door while we were talking in the hallway, but her husband insisted the door remain open. He said he wanted to hear his son's footsteps when he returned."

"Go reinterview the boy's parents. Maybe, just maybe, you'll get them to separate."

"Hey, Sarge, you'll want to see this," a voice from the kitchen shouted.

Carlson placed his five on his desk and followed Lawrence into the small kitchen. A large twenty-four-inch box Sylvania black-and-white television sat on top of the GE Frost-Free Refrigerator. Detective Jim Hegerty reached up to turn the volume knob up so all could see and hear. "Hey, boss, the line should start in about fifteen minutes, by tomorrow, the line will be around the station house. It looks like 1 PP gave it to the press. Pictures and all," Hegerty said.

Sergeant Lawrence shook his head in disgust, as he looked at the taped interview with the police commissioner. "They could have at least given me a heads-up."

"Tell the cop assigned to the apartment not to say a word to the press. Everything said now about the missing boy will have to be cleared with the 'Building,'" Lawrence said. Carlson dumped his cold cup of coffee into the sink. "There goes my reinterviews of the parents."

"No need to, the boy's father already gave an interview. He said what he needed to say," Hegerty said with a smirk.

"Let's have some quiet in here," Lawrence said as four other detectives squeezed into the small room.

The detectives listened for two minutes before the telephone in the sergeant's office began to ring.

"Hey, Vin, see who that is. I wanna hear this. Jim, make some mental notes of the Zapata statements."

Carlson squeezed between the last two detectives and made his way to Lawrence's office and picked up the heavy receiver. He listened for a few moments, he wrote some notes on a blank sheet of yellow legal paper. He folded the paper and walked back to the crowded kitchen. The television was now turned off, and the detectives had made their way back to their desks. Carlson and Lawrence remained in the kitchen. Carlson handed the paper to his boss.

9

Anniversaries Should Only Be for Marriages

Four Months Later
First Precinct Detective Squad Room
0700 Hours

Detective Carlson finished signing into the detective squad sign-in log, he moved the ruler to between the next two lines below and drew a line across the entire page. He tossed the ruler onto the page and closed the book. He looked into his boss's office. Sergeant Lawrence was on the telephone talking with his new girlfriend. His boss moved differently as he talked with different people and no two had the same gyrations. He looked over to Hegerty. "I saw the report on the four-month anniversary of the Zapata case, any more people wanting to give themselves up?" Carlson asked.

"Nothing for about a week, we are still at seventy-two people who are willing to confess to the boy's disappearance," Sergeant Lawrence said as he walked past Carlson and went into the kitchen. The coffee was ready. "Seven have come in over five times to renew their request to surrender," Lawrence said as he poured the coffee into his already dirty coffee cup. He looked at it sideways. *I can't remember when I cleaned it last,* he thought.

"How long will I remain as the lead detective? My girlfriend says I'm ready to settle down again," Carlson said.

Lawrence took a short sip of the very hot coffee. "It's the natural order of life, police work at its finest."

"That was a good one. Practiced it for a while?" Carlson said.

"About a week," Lawrence said after another short sip.

"Sarge, there has been a surge in the number of street robberies. How about I take a few cases, just to keep my mind active. I can't keep reading and rereading the fives on the Zapata kid."

"Okay, but if anything comes up on the kid, you'll have to drop whatever you are doing and pick it up later."

"This latest group of rehires was great but with no real training support," Carlson said. "The PC liked the concept but said it would be detrimental to the new kids coming directly out of the Academy. He wanted them to be trained in groups by a sergeant directly."

"The most active guys from this last group were to be used to train the next group of rehires after them. Since this is the last group of cops who were laid off, the precincts will get the real 'rookies' right out of the academy in a few weeks. I could train the rookies. Most of the new training guys are the sergeant's drivers and not qualified to train," Carlson said.

"Hey, you were my driver for a time," Lawrence said.

“Not for nothing, Sarge, but I hated driving you. Go here, do this, you were a pain to drive. Say, when are you going to make lieutenant and take over the squad?” Carlson said.

The telephone on Carlson’s desk began to ring. He answered it. “First squad, Carlson. Yeah okay, I got it. No one goes in, not even the patrol sergeant.” He put his receiver on its cradle. Carlson turned to his boss’s office door and shouted. “Hey, Sarge, we got a homicide, real messy. I’ll get the car,” Carlson said as he pulled the sergeant’s RMP keys from the board. It was a white board with black street lines and block designations on it, as well as hooks for each unmarked RMP key ring, with a metal disc with the car number. It made it easy to find an unmarked car in an emergency.

Sergeant Lawrence mimicked Carlson in a low voice, “Oh, Sarge, I’ll get the car. A minute ago, I was the world’s biggest pain in the ass. Things do change quickly around here.”

Thirteenth Precinct Station House – Muster Room

The process of acclimating the police officers, who were laid off on June 30, 1975, at 0000 hours, back into policing, was initially difficult, at best. The rehires started to return in groups of two to three hundred. They were “senior” rookie cops with three to four years of prior service. Joyce’s group consisted of almost a thousand cops who had a year or less of service. They were the next to last group to be rehired. Now it was time for them to leave their NSU and go patrol precincts. Sergeant Gregory held the blue sheet of paper which covered their orders.

"Listen up, I have the orders for your new assignments. I am only going to read off the assignments for those of you here. I will make phone calls to the others. Sergeants Jaffee and Reynolds are calling their people as I speak. I do want to say that I am very proud of everything we accomplished. I think NSU II has been utilized at more strikes, demonstrations, parades then all the others combined."

"Yeah, like the Yankees ticker-tape parade," someone said.

The sergeant smiled. "Yeah, Joyce got the most free feels in his life. We had the truck with all the Yankees on it. The girls wanted to get close and Joyce and the rest of us had to move them back," another officer said. The group laughed and high-fived each other including the five women.

"Okay, now listen up: this is your last tour in the NSU, you will report to your new commands on Monday. I know tomorrow should be your last day, but you can come in whenever you like to get your gear and a locker in your new commands," Gregory said.

"Here are your new commands: Allen, you'll stay here in the Thirteenth. Bini to the One-Two-Three. Brown to the Sixth. Joyce to the Ninth, I guess your activity got you there. Martinez to the Seventh. Murphy to the Firearms Training Unit. Nice gig . . . etc. Peterson to the Sixth. Thompson to the Communications Section. Williams and Vasquez to the Tenth. Zuccarelli to the Fifth."

I have a list of the important stuff we did: Yes, the Yankees winning the World Series, and the ticker-tape parade up Broadway. The USA Hockey Team winning the Olympic gold medal and their parade up Broadway. The Pope's visit. The Racetrack Strike. Fourth of July Yacht Club Security. Thanksgiving Parade Barrier detail. The Wall Street Explosion. The search for Little Nate Zapata, the FIRST night.

"If I forgot something, please write it down and send it to: Who really gives a shit, care of Patrol Borough Manhattan South."

"This will be the last time I will be saying this to all of you. You have made me proud of all of you. I hope some of you make sergeant, some more to lieutenant, and others to captains and higher. I cannot say this any stronger, if you desire to go higher, you will need to get a college degree. John Jay College is an option. Now pick up your gear and make the most of your careers, more importantly, make a difference out there. Thank you for being the people you are, and for protecting the people out there. Always remember, your family comes first, then 'The Job.'"

They all stood and applauded the sergeant, then they formed a line to shake his hand. Joyce waited for everyone to leave the muster room.

"Ya know, Sarge, I just wish we could have found that little boy from SoHo. It would have been our 'last-second' touchdown in a Super Bowl or that walk-off home run at the final game of the World Series. We had a good, no, a great team of guys and gals. We were a microcosm of the city's population. White males and females, black males and females, Hispanic males and females, most married, others singles, we were 'an all-in-one package,'" Joyce said.

"Bob, you gave up the most by coming back to the job. You were the former vice president of the United States bodyguard. You went all over the world with him and his family, and you still held out your loyalty. You'll never hear it from us, but even the borough commander knows what you gave up to be back here, and you were my top, go to guy."

"Yeah, boss, but I never found that little boy from SoHo. I wanted to find him so badly, for his parents, for the city, for me."

"Bob, look, I couldn't say this to the troops at roll call, but tonight at eighteen hundred hours, I am throwing a good-bye party for the both crews. I would appreciate it if you could contact the guys who were not here this morning and tell them the party will be at the Village Conference House. I will be there, will you?" Gregory asked.

"Sarge, I will be there and even if it is only you and I. I will be proud to sit and have a drink with you."

The Village Conference House

The Sixth Precinct was a popular place for people to go and enjoy a Friday or Saturday night drinking. This party was for cops and cops only. Joyce had called his wife and told her about the Ninth Precinct, omitting the fact that so many cops had been killed in the line of duty. He made it look like the old lower east side, rather than the retail drug capital of the world. Gregory held his bottle of beer in his shooting hand, something that Joyce noticed but kept out of their conversation. The conversation immediately turned to the little boy from SoHo.

"Bob, this will probably be my last time I talk about this. I have to talk to you about the Zapata case, but the information is for me, and me only."

"Boss, what do you want to know?" Joyce asked.

"What do you think happened to Nate Zapata?" Gregory asked.

"Boss, I don't have specific proof, so I won't put it on paper. I do believe I know who did it and that person or persons have already been interviewed by the detectives."

"Are you telling me that the parents killed their own son?"

"Sarge, I'm saying I can't rule them out. It's just that their story doesn't fit. Like a lie a perp says to you when you are about to put the cuffs on them." Bini grabbed Joyce from the sergeant and they began to dance. The other cops soon followed.

The party lasted until after midnight. Joyce, Gregory, Bini, and others cleaned up the spills and put everything into thick black garbage bags. No one would ever know the cops had a party at the conference house. Like the murder on Prince Street.

10

How the Other Half Lives Ninth Precinct – Manhattan's Lower East Side

Joyce stood in front of the large oak desk which showed its age. The plaques with the photos of the officers killed in the line of duty stared down at everyone in the "Muster Room." There was a small room just behind Joyce, and to his left, it was designated as the youth room. The COs' office door was to Joyce's left and in front of him just around the desk. The TS and the radio room was to his right. The prisoner processing area was in the far back room of the precinct. The community affairs office was out the door which was to Joyce's back, down three steps to the left and into the crudely constructed office. That was originally the barn for the horses when they were used by patrol. This building was built in 1909.

"Hey, kid, can you walk the four flights of stairs to your locker?" Terry Ryan said. He had a crusty voice of a sailor but the heart of a priest. His first duty was always to the desk sergeant. Then it was to the cops new to the precinct. Ryan would buy the prisoners a sandwich if they missed the prisoner meal run. Terry was just five feet eight inches, he had more salt than pepper in his hair. He had very thin frame with the courage of a terrier.

The elevator hadn't worked in fifty years. The stairs consisted of twelve very worn original steps. Then a platform, a rest area for some overweight cops, then another twelve steps and Joyce was on the second floor. *Two more flights to go,* he thought. He grabbed his gear and raced up the stairs. He had been training for the NYC Marathon. He reached the top floor or so he thought. The stairs continued up another flight. Joyce waited for Ryan, who was sweating, but not out of breath, as he put his foot on the fourth-floor platform. Joyce looked up the stairs as Terry stood. "Hey, Terry, what's up there?" Joyce asked.

"That is a very lonely place but with interesting views. Up there is the gym. Not too many guys use it, but after watching you climb, I guess you will be taking advantage of it."

"Terry, I will be running the marathon this October. I ran Long Island but didn't finish so well."

"What was your time?"

"Five hours, twenty-eight minutes, and seventeen seconds."

"You know the freaken' seconds."

"It was my first, you always remember your first," Joyce said.

"I remember my first broad but that's it," Terry said and began to cough.

"See you always remember your first," Joyce replied.

There was an empty locker in the far corner of the locker room right by the windows. The six-foot-high window frames held the single-paned glass in place. "No shades?" Joyce asked.

“Hey, kid, I’ve been here twenty-five years and there has never been any need for shades and the windows are never closed, even in the winter, and it never gets cold up here. It is noisy as hell but never cold with the steam pipes banging all day and night long,” Terry said.

Joyce opened his locker. He was pleased that the previous owner didn’t leave behind a pile of garbage, nor did he leave behind a pile of money. He hung his uniforms on the bar across the center of the locker. His personal items went on the shelf along with his service revolver wrapped in a silicone cloth. He hung his duty belt on a coat hook and pushed his spare pair of shoes onto the bottom of the locker. He pulled his combination lock from his belt, slammed the locker door, and slid the neck of the combination lock through the small hole. He engaged the lock and pulled, it was secure.

“Now let’s get you down to payroll and time records, but first let’s peek in at roll call. They will put you into a spot that you should like. One of our guys was transferred out last night under a cloud. No one in his squad knows he went missing yet. He had the holiday squad,” Terry said. Joyce looked at him with a puzzled expression. Terry grabbed his arm and walked him into the small roll call room.

“Hey, girls, this is Bobby Joyce. He was one of the rehired guys who were laid off and put into one of those NSU teams. He needs a squad and I happen to know that Bill Murphy’s transfer came through at midnight. Give Bobby his spot.”

“He’s the only one who had expressed interest in that squad, so it’s his spot, welcome to the Ninth,” Tunisha Brown said and smiled at her “new meat.”

The First Day of Patrol in the Ninth

It had been a few years since Joyce had been on patrol. His first command was the Seven-O in Brooklyn. Midnights were murderous, not in the sense of too much work, but in the Seven-O there was no work. There could be one call for service for the entire set of five tours and that was for the entire command. The hard part was trying to stay awake for the eight hours. He was about to see how the other half lived. Joyce slid into the white RMP, put his hat on the rear seat, pulled his gun belt so his holstered revolver was over his groin. He slammed his memo book between the windshield and the dashboard. His portable radio was in its holder. Gone were the telephone receivers which hung on the dashboard. It was used to acknowledge the calls for service, from the radio dispatcher, known as "Central."

"Nine Adam on the air," Central called. Joyce's partner Angel Padilla, a five-year veteran of the precinct, waited for three seconds.

"That's us, Rook," Padilla said.

"Jeez, we just got in the car," Joyce said and picked up the "mike."

"Nine Adam," Joyce responded.

"Nine Adam, respond to a ten-ten drug sales at 908 East Eighth Street," the dispatcher said. Joyce grabbed his memo book and wrote in the job.

"Hey, Rook, you don't need to put every job in your memo book, just the important ones," Padilla said as he continued to drive.

"I do it my way, you do it yours, and I'm not a freaken' rookie," Joyce said.

"Gotcha, Rook," Padilla said, without looking over at him.

Joyce learned from his training officers, "Never look over to your partner when you are having a conversation. Always have your eyes looking around at the people on the street. Your partner will always be there to hear you."

"Hey, kid, after this job, I'll show you the precinct and then sectors Adam and Boy. They are the smallest but they are the busiest in the city, trust me on that."

"I heard there are a lot of drugs here."

"The drugs are everywhere. I'll show the spots but don't write them down, just memorize them."

"I like to make collars," Joyce said

"I did for the first five years. Now I let the rookies have them," Padilla said.

Padilla drove the car slowly west bound on the street, against traffic which was practically nonexistent. The curbs were lined with autos stripped clean, most of the buildings were abandoned, but none were boarded up. Their car pulled up to the location. It was a typical Lower East Side five-story, two-hallway apartment house. All its windows were intact. The ground and second floor windows had bars on them. Fire escapes ran from the ground floor to the fifth floor on both sides of the building. A large door allowed access to the foyer to call to the apartments for entry. Joyce reached behind him and grabbed his eight-point uniform hat.

"Hey, Rook, this is the Ninth, we don't wear our hats."

"I do," Joyce said as he looked up at the building.

"We get five calls a tour for this location."

"Do you ever go into the building or just give it a ninety x-ray and keep on going?" Joyce asked.

"I guess we are going into the building," Padilla said as he looked up at the cloudy sky and said, "Lord, why me."

Padilla took his time getting out of their patrol car. Joyce whispered, "Hey, Angel, what's up."

"Just giving them time to gather their shit and scram, then we make it a ninety x-ray."

Suddenly a woman came storming out of the building. "When the hell are you cops ever going inside the building? The drug dealers are not out here, they are, or at least they were, in the lobby. They don't live in the building but they harass us tenants all day long. We have one of the good buildings on this entire block, both sides. They come into our lobby because they feel safe there. If you came quicker after you stopped, you would have surprised them. They never run until you get out of the car but then you always take your time to go inside. If you stopped twenty feet back and rushed inside, you would catch them with their drugs, but nooo, you take your sweet time and they simply pack up their shit and run out the back door, into the rear yard. We have no fences around this building and the lock to the front door is always broken, no keys needed."

"Now we can go in," Padilla said.

Joyce unholstered his Smith and Wesson six-shot revolver and put it into his hat. His index finger was on the trigger. They slowly walked into the building. The woman walked to the curb and leaned against their patrol car. "You're too late, they are gone," she said.

"Hey, you never know. They may have left some product on the floor," Joyce said.

"Doubt it but let's have a look," Padilla said.

Now he wants to look when it's safe, Joyce thought. They walked inside, "Stay outside until it's safe," Joyce said innocently to the woman.

"I live here. I know the dealers and they know me. My husband used to be the building super but he died from a drug overdose, so I took over cleaning the building to keep my apartment," she said, still leaning against their car but now had her arms folded against her stomach.

"Please stay out here until I say to come in," Joyce said. Padilla smiled and shook his head.

"Yes, sir, mister officer," the woman said sarcastically.

Joyce entered the lobby and did a visual sweep. Then he checked the stairwells, no noise, he knew they were gone for the moment. The floors and walls were clean for a lobby. Joyce wondered what the other floors would look like upon inspection.

"It's clean," Joyce said to his partner.

"Of course it's clean. The dealers are gone and I just finished mopping the floors ten minutes ago," the woman said.

Joyce went to put his hat on when the woman grabbed his arm. "That picture of the boy, is he your son?" she asked.

"No, he's just a boy who went missing about four months ago."

"He's a good-looking boy, I've seen him before," she said.

"Where?"

"Here, right in this building. He always came with a woman who said she was his aunt, but I know she was a junkie. I have not seen the boy with her in months."

"What apartment did she go to?"

"4-B but they, well, moved out. Let's just say their shit was moved out about a month ago so the landlord could repaint the apartment and rent it out. They were four, you know, faggots. They liked little boys. They always talked about doing it, you know, to little boys," she said.

"Do you know the woman's name?" Joyce asked.

"No, I never talked to her but I gave her an evil look when she brought the boy over here on Fridays."

"Fridays, why Fridays?" Joyce asked.

"They, the faggots, worked in the area and always got paid on a Friday. The woman would drop the boy off at the apartment and leave with a big smile on her face. I knew what she was up to. That poor little boy."

"The woman, what did she look like?" Joyce asked.

"My height, dirty brown hair, skinny, junkie skinny, a few teeth missing. She smelled," the woman said.

"Hey, partner, I gotta give this job back, they're holding jobs," Padilla said. He was the driver and Joyce was the recorder, the cop who answered the calls for service.

"Do you have the names of the men in the apartment?" Joyce asked.

"What are you going to do for me?" the woman asked coyly.

"I'll be back in two hours. Have the names for me and I will have what you want," Joyce said coldly.

"No, I don't do sex, you can die from those diseases," she said.

Joyce smiled at the woman and then gently held her hand. He suddenly tightened his grip and slid the sleeve of the woman's thin blouse up, exposing her fresh track marks.

"Have the names for me in two hours, we will be back," Joyce said.

"Okay, I can get them for you right away."

"You have twenty seconds," Joyce said softly.

The woman ran into her apartment and returned in fifteen seconds, with her copy of the listing of the men and their social security numbers. She scowled at Joyce.

"You have their names, now what?"

Joyce whispered something into her ear. She remained frozen until the two cops walked out of her building. The door to the building closed behind them. He slipped into their RMP when the woman let out a scream.

"What the hell was that all about?" Padilla asked.

"Nothing, just a rookie thing. Let's resume, I want to see more of the precinct's drug operations."

"It's your first day, Rook, relax," Padilla said.

11

You Never Know Manhattan District Attorney's Office

Sarah Wasserman was the district attorney assigned to one of Joyce's gun cases. He had been assigned to crowd control at an HBO film shoot, of a music dance club while he was assigned to NSU II. He arrested two Westies for gun possession that night. Wasserman sat at her desk in a half metal, half glass enclosure with an officemate. Files were piled on her floor but a chair had been left empty. Wasserman sported a white gold wedding band which encased an engagement ring. Joyce's wedding finger was blank. Wasserman stood all of five feet three inches, but had the heart of an NBA basketball player. She was rough on her defendants but rougher on her cops.

"Officer, tell me again how you came to be assigned to this security detail duty?" Wasserman asked.

"My wife wanted me to go with her to our daughter's doctor. My tours usually ran until two in the morning and the appointment for her doctor was for eight thirty that morning. I had some lost time built up, so I decided to take the last two hours of my tour off. My sergeant decided to use me as security at this HBO event. It was to be an easy gig, until the Irish mob showed up. Someone told me that there might be trouble in the hallway leading to the studio, so I decided to take a peek. The next thing I knew, someone shouted, 'They got guns,' and all hell broke loose. I saw some guys pushing violently through the crowd, so I followed them."

"Did you say or shout, 'Police, don't move or drop your weapons,' that sort of stuff?"

"Nope, I just followed them, that was until I saw one guy toss what appeared to be a Smith and Wesson Chief under a car. He separated from the other three. I hoped he was now unarmed. He turned and saw me approaching and he bolted down the street. I chased him for a half a block. I grabbed him and pushed him against a brick wall. I searched him and came up with a .32 semi-automatic pistol with a silencer stuffed in his drawers. I cuffed him," Joyce said.

"Then, what did you do?" Wasserman said.

"I dragged the prick back to the car where I saw him toss his other pistol, by that time backup arrived and I handed my prisoner to one of the officers while I went under the car and retrieved the other pistol."

"That will be your grand jury testimony. Anything else?" Wasserman said.

Joyce reached into the inside pocket of his corduroy sport coat and removed a sheet of paper. He had made a copy of the list of names and social security numbers the woman had given him. He handed the paper to Wasserman. "Could you do me a big favor and check on these names and see if any of them had ever been arrested, possibly for sex crimes?"

"Is it a personal matter?"

"No, not really, I have a suspicion, but I don't know where to go with it right now."

"I'll take the list and see what I can do. I have grand jury all day. It may take a week or two. For now, let's go indict some Westies."

Ninth Precinct
One week later

Joyce sat in the juvenile holding room as he waited for the sergeant to make the final changes to the Third Platoon roll call.

"All right, everyone, fall in for roll call," the sergeant called out.

The muster room was now crowded with uniformed cops. The anticrime cops stood alongside the sergeant. They all had hair to down their shoulders. A color of the day headband was displayed on each undercover cop. Once outside the precinct, the band was removed and positioned on their wrists or on their pants' belt loop. A long button-down shirt was worn to conceal their holstered weapon, a .38 cal. Smith and Wesson five-shot revolver. Terry Ryan was seated at the TS or telephone switchboard post.

When Joyce started at the Seven-O, they had a true switchboard with cords and switches to pull. He had no clue as what to do. One day the desk sergeant ordered him to take the seat while the TS operator went to the bathroom. He saw a switch that had been pushed forward. He moved it back into its upright position. Two seconds the captain walked out of his office and went straight to the sergeant and ripped him apart. Two minutes later, Joyce was walking a foot post alone. He had disconnected the captain, who had been talking with his midnight squeeze.

Terry Ryan looked up from the roll call sign-out sheet and waved it to get Joyce's attention. Terry whispered something to the sergeant. "Joyce, fall out, there is a DA looking for you."

A few comments later and Joyce was through the five rows of cops and over at the TS.

"Terry, what's up?" Joyce asked.

He held his hand over the mouthpiece of the telephone. Long gone were the cords and switches.

"I got a DA on the line, do you want to talk to her?"

"I'll take it, kind of expecting it," Joyce said and took the handset. "Officer Joyce here."

"Officer, you hit a home run on the names you gave me. They have all been convicted of numerous sex offenses. There is good news, they are all dead."

Joyce looked down for a moment, then he smiled. "Thanks for the info."

"How about a drink some night?" she asked.

"I'm married," he said softly.

"So am I."

12

Life Goes On, or Does It First Precinct Detective Squad Room

Sergeant Lawrence pulled the case folder from his "out" box and put it in front of him. The four-inch-thick Nate Zapata case file had stopped growing. The lieutenant in the chief of detectives had asked Lawrence for an update on the Zapata case as the commissioner's office had requested.

"Hey, Vin, how do we stand on the Zapata case?" Lawrence shouted to the still lead detective.

"Boss, we have come up empty of the kid. I interviewed the parents of all the kids listed as taking the same yellow school bus which stopped at the curb on West Broadway. The parents remembered the morning he, Nate Zapata, supposedly went missing, but none could remember seeing Nate at the bus stop. Most of the parents said they would have been surprised to see Nate walking alone to the school bus stop. Once the report that Nate had gone missing went out to the public, they told me they called each other and none of them could remember seeing Nate that morning.

"One parent did say that an off-duty cop did talk with her and a few other mothers a few weeks after the first report of the boy who had gone missing," Carlson said.

Sergeant Lawrence put his folder on his desk and opened it. It was Carlson's five on the last parents' interview. He held it in his hand but didn't open it. He walked out of his office to Carlson's desk and placed the manila folder on top of Carlson's notes.

"I'm guessing it was one of the NSU 'kids' who was there that first night. I talked with him on the phone. He told me his sergeant assigned him and his partner to do a little ghosting of possible witnesses. I guess the 'kid' is no rookie, he had the same idea as this office of seasoned detectives had. I like him," Lawrence said.

"Why would his sergeant do that?" Carlson asked as he opened the folder.

"To make some points with the borough commander. If the *kid* found the boy before we did, he and his partner would be given their golden ticket."

"We're on the same team," Carlson said angrily.

"Not when it comes to promotions, then it becomes a catfight. I did some checking on my own and I discovered that the sergeant comes from a long line of firemen," Lawrence said.

"Why don't the rubber men play their games with each other and leave the real work to the professionals," Carlson said.

"I have a meeting with the chief this morning. Anything I should know about?"

"See if he could give the okay to having the parents take a lie detector test," Carlson said quickly.

"I'll ask the chief but it's got to be voluntary," Lawrence said.

"I know we.... but we need to eliminate them. Oh by the way, I'd go up there wearing my cheapest suit, because he's going to rip you to shreds," Carlson said.

"The chief will probably have to run it by 'The Building,' so we have a week or so to get someone lined that can be vetted," Lawrence said

"There is that retired lieutenant out on Long Island who works with the Nassau and Suffolk County Police Departments. He does most of their testing. I understand he is quite good. We can do it here," Carlson said.

Ninth Precinct
Later That Night

It was the start of the dreaded midnight tours for Joyce. To compound the atmosphere, the weather was unusually warm for a September night. It was also a Friday night into a Saturday morning. Those who lived inside the five-story tenements would be lined up against the abandoned cars along the curb, some sitting on the stoops, others had chairs to sit on as they played Dominos on a three-foot-by-three-foot square piece of plywood, which had been placed atop an overturned garbage can. The people on the streets had their cold bottles of Heineken beer wrapped in a small brown paper bag, either in their hand or at their feet. Sergeant Kramer and Greico stood in front of the desk. Kramer was taller and heavier than his fellow sergeant. The borough ordered all precincts in Manhattan to have two sergeants working patrol during the unexpected heat wave. The Ninth was susceptible to a spontaneous combustion when an arrest was made and the cops needed to use some street justice to control a suspect. Grieco was a runner and couldn't wait to talk with Joyce who was running in the upcoming NYC Marathon.

Sergeant Grieco started. "Fall in for roll call," he said.

"Joyce, you and Puccio have sector Adam/Boy."

Puccio let out a long breath of air. He was a steady "Late Tour" cop who liked to ride alone in his "one-man" scooter. A letter had been dropped on him saying that he was spending his entire tour sleeping with his Puerto Rican girlfriend, whom some cops thought was a drug dealer. Puccio started to shuffle his feet. "They're screwing me," he moaned.

"Hey, Poochie, not getting any squeeze time tonight?" one officer said to the enjoyment of all.

Later
Inside Their Patrol Car

There was a crowd of people in the middle of the intersection of Avenue D and East Eighth Street. They began to signal for the officers to come over. "If it's a fight, the ones who are waving to us are the ones backing the guy who is losing," Puccio said casually.

Joyce put on the overhead lights. There was a young girl lying on the ground, a small stream of blood came from the side of her head. Joyce stepped out of their car when someone yelled, "She's been shot."

Joyce pulled his portable radio out of its holder and began, "Nine Adam to Central K."

"Go, Nine Adam," the dispatcher said calmly.

"Central, Nine and D, female shot, have a 'bus' respond forthwith." Joyce holstered his portable radio, while Puccio moved the crowd back. Joyce felt for the girl's pulse, there was none. "I'm gonna try CPR," Joyce shouted.

Joyce pushed the girl's head back and his hand was immediately full of blood. He pinched her nose and tried two breaths—nothing. He let her head drop back and slid his fingers down between her breasts and felt for her breastbone. He slid his bloodied middle finger over the spot. He wouldn't have to waste time trying to find the spot again. He started the fifteen compressions, he stopped at fifteen. He tried three more breaths—nothing. He put his right hand over the red spot and tried again. He heard the sirens. Three more breaths and the siren got louder. He checked her pulse as the scream of the sirens of the ambulance let Joyce know that help had arrived.

The paramedics pushed through the crowd and dropped their canvass bag to the girl's side. "I got it, I got her pulse," Joyce said to Danny, a paramedic he had worked with prior to his becoming a cop. They worked together connecting the central office switching systems for the telephone company at the World Trade Center.

Joyce walked over to the flow of water coming from a running fire hydrant and washed the blood off his hands. He went into the glove compartment of his RMP and took out a handful of napkins and dried off his hands. He turned to see a large Hispanic man trying to push the paramedics away from the girl. Joyce knew if they were not allowed to continue, the girl would go into cardiac arrest. Joyce pulled the man away.

"Sir, please don't interfere with the paramedics, I got the girl's heart beating again. If you interrupt them, she is sure to die and you will have to take that guilt to the grave," Joyce said. The man's arms relaxed.

"I came down to see if she was my daughter. My wife sent her out to the bodega to get her numbers. My wife is confined to bed and her numbers are all that she has to look forward to."

The paramedics were wrapping the girl's head with gauze. Joyce slid his index and middle finger into the girl's rear pants pockets. He pulled out a slip of paper and balled it up before walking away. Joyce handed the man the slip of paper.

"Here is the slip of paper. Now leave the paramedics alone, by the way, what is your daughter's name?"

"She is a neighbor, we call her 'Tina.' Her parents work in the evenings and my wife takes care of her. I will get you the information you need, sorry I lied to you," he said.

Joyce looked back to him, "Never lie to me again," Joyce said coldly.

An unmarked detective's car pulled to the location. The crowd moved back to the sidewalks. The street was now completely open. The patrol sergeant pulled to the scene and stepped out of his car. "Puccio, it's yours. Joyce, you remain in sector Adam/Boy, I'll get you a partner, oh by the way, nice work."

"Hey, Sarge, how did you know I did what I did?"

"You still have some blood on the tip of your nose, Puccio was clean as a whistle, that's why I gave it to him." Joyce didn't say another word.

Joyce noticed the woman who had been standing on the fringe of the crowd had started to walk toward him. "Officer Joyce, we meet again, it has been a while," the woman said.

"I heard that those four men died suddenly, and all at the same time, from an overdose," Joyce said softly.

"Officer, I have no idea what you are talking about," the woman said and smiled coyly.

"You did the community a great service, but I just wish you would have let me talk to them before you gave them your own version of a happy meal. I wanted to ask them about the woman who brought the little boy to them. Was she paid and how much? More importantly, what did those men do to him?" Joyce said.

"I saw the picture of the boy in the newspaper, just like the one you keep in your hat," she said.

"The detectives probably ran into a wall, so they will throw the boy's picture out as a reminder to the public. By the way, has the woman been back?" Joyce asked.

"Yes, but with another little boy. That's why it happened. I may be a junkie but I know what they were doing to that little boy was wrong and they had to be stopped."

"I need the woman's name," Joyce said.

"I don't know her real name, no one uses their real name on the street," the woman said.

"I understand that, but I was hoping she may have given it to you accidentally. You still owe me for the package. Keep your eyes open. If you find out her name, let me know immediately," Joyce said.

"Like who shot the girl. It was supposed to be a drug rip-off. Two guys from Second Street tried to rip off the manager of Blue Tape Dope. They tried to shoot him as he was walking back with all the money but missed him and hit the girl. She's going to be all right, isn't she?" the woman asked.

"She is dead."

13

Not All Parallels Are Equal
Chief of Detective's Office

Sergeant Lawrence sat along the fake wall paneling in a preformed chair made of metal and plastic. SPAA Bronwinski put her telephone receiver down in its cradle and looked at Lawrence. "Sergeant, the chief will see you. Go right through the last door on the right."

Lawrence entered and sat in the lone chair in front of the chief of detectives.

"Sergeant, it's good to see you in person. I have seen you many times on the TV."

"Thanks, boss."

"I have read over your request to have the parents of the little boy interviewed, is there anything you want to add?" the chief asked.

"Nothing, boss, except, well, er, it's actually for the parents to take a lie detector test," Lawrence said.

"I've run it by the First Dep and he gave me the okay. I will grant you the permission to interview both the parents. I like the way you referred to the test as an interview. I hope no one picks up on it," the chief said.

"Boss, there is a possibility of a parallel investigation in the works," Lawrence said.

"How the hell did that happen?" the chief said angrily.

"It started with an NSU II sergeant, he has recently retired. He had one of his sharpest cops do a parallel investigation on the Zapata case," Lawrence said.

"Have you talked with this officer?" the chief asked.

"Yes, I have. I believe he developed a new source and is keeping it close to his vest," Lawrence said.

"I want his source," the chief said sternly.

Ninth Precinct
Another Late-Night Tour

Puccio had become increasingly anxious as Joyce drove the remainder of the tour. He constantly checked his watch. He had Joyce drive on East Fourth Street eight times in the last hour.

"Hey, Puch, you seem kind of restless tonight," Joyce said.

"Man, the woman you talked to at the shooting, the other night, she's either a drug dealer or a pros."

"She is a junkie like eighty percent of the women down here. She supports her habit by working as a building super."

"Yeah, but she walked up to you like you and she just did it the night before."

"I'll leave the trashy work to you and let's leave it at that," Joyce said and smiled.

"She just seemed . . . way too friendly."

"She owes me big time. She thought she was doing the right thing by taking out four scummers," Joyce said.

"Oh, you mean the four boy bangers who just happened to OD at the same time in the same apartment," Puccio said casually. "Bobby, you already have a reputation here in the Ninth. It didn't take long for that to happen," Puccio added.

"I let my reputation work for me. The bigger, the more dangerous, and terrible it gets, the easier it is to make collars without having to fight a perp. I have enough replacement teeth to make a dentist want to retire."

"So the story of you throwing that nine-month pregnant woman out the window was just bullshit?" Puccio asked.

"I will never admit to anything but I simply let the rep keep going and building," Joyce said.

Joyce pulled into the precinct block. "Bobby, pull in, I'm gonna check with the sergeant to see if I can get some lost time."

"Your girlfriend on Fourth Street horny again?"

"Hey, how do you know?"

"Your yellow Ford Pinto sitting in the illegal spot and your scooter sitting behind the dumpster all night is a dead giveaway. Did you get a discount for the color? It looks like a cab."

14

Liar, Liar
Staten Island

Joyce sat in his favorite booth in Joyce's Eltingville Inn. The Irish fiddler played some of his typical Irish rebel songs as he and Carol listened. It had been a while since they sat and talked. They laughed when the conversation made a left turn and Joyce started with the Zapata case.

"Bob, since we last worked together that night, have you ever thought about anything else?"

"Actually I do, but it seems when we get together, all I think about is that little boy. I still carry his picture in my hat, just in case."

"Just in case of what, that you are wrong in your thinking? Can that be true?" Carol said jokingly and held his hand gently.

"It's nice when we can get together after a four by twelve rather than a six to two thirty, where the bartender is pissed that you showed up and made his night longer," Joyce said softly. She let his hand go, but still looked into his eyes.

"I happen to enjoy the company," Bini said.

"You know, I like the music, but once they start playing, we have to talk louder. I just have to keep one ear to the music and the other to our conversation."

"We agreed this would be better than trying to have a private conversation over the telephone, without any interruptions," Bini said.

"I appreciate your coming out," he said.

"So what's bothering you?" she said.

"The Zapata kid. There are just too many things that don't fit into any of the open spaces in the puzzle."

"Like what?"

"Like, I'm still getting phone hang-ups after my tours. My wife swears that she has not had one in years," Joyce said.

"The other thing . . . the Zapata boy was allowed to go to school for the very first time by himself, in the city of New York, alone. Supposedly under the careful watch of his mother. We proved that his mother didn't walk behind him to the school bus stop. Then we proved that she could not have watched him walk all the way to his school bus stop from his apartment house. That's the first piece that doesn't fit. It wasn't a city bus stop but a location where the yellow school bus would stop and take the kids to Zapata's school. We know that none of the other parents, who also had their children traveling with Nate, saw the boy that morning."

"Two . . . the parents wait until almost until six in the evening to report their son missing, and everyone is okay with that. Really?"

"That freaken' bitch will catch a close grouping from me if I ever meet her," Bini said angrily.

"After Nate went missing, the cousin changed over to another little boy but the men she was supposed to bring the new boy to, went suddenly dead."

"Bob, did you have anything to do with it?"

"No, but I know who did, and that's between us."

"I can see your frustration. Have the detectives given the parents a lie detector test yet?" she asked.

"I am not certain, they have kept things close and out of the press. Even if they do, the parents could take a Quaalude and it would relax them enough to pass. I will watch for the newspapers if they do. By the way, how are the kids doing?"

"They are always asking why I have to work. I'd hate to tell them work is my relief from my husband. You never heard that from me. By the way, my husband shot blanks while we were on vacation," she said with a smile.

The Zapatas' Apartment

Alan Zapata slammed the black corded telephone into its cradle then pushed his hands into the back pockets of his jeans.

"Alan, what's the matter?" Arlene asked softly.

"The police want us to take a polygraph or a lie detector test as they call it. They say they just want to clear us so they can continue with their investigation."

"What are we going to do, should we hire a lawyer?"

"We can't afford a criminal lawyer, besides, how would we look if we hired a lawyer? It would suggest that we are guilty or somehow we had something to do with Nate's disappearance."

"But we did, we did or at least you did, you killed our son and disposed of his body."

Alan wanted to scream, but he knew the concrete floors and walls would only amplify his shouts. He needed to end this conversation.

"We have to do it, I mean, we have to take the test, and without a lawyer. Trust me, we can do this," he said softly.

First Precinct Squad Room

Detective Carlson slowly returned the receiver to its cradle and stared at the telephone. Detective Joseph sat at his desk and allowed Carlson a few moments after the call.

"Hey, Vin, what's up?" Joseph asked.

Carlson turned to his "partner for the day" and had a quizzical look on his face. He picked up his coffee mug and walked into the kitchen to retrieve another cup of stale coffee. "They agreed to take the lie detector test," Carlson said from the kitchen.

"They? Who agreed to take a lie detector test and for what?" Joseph asked.

"The Zapatas, and they don't want a lawyer present either."

"I'd be jumping up and down if it were my case, though they certainly seem like they had nothing to do with their son's disappearance," Joseph said.

"I don't know. I still want to have another talk with that cop from the Ninth," Carlson said.

The Next Afternoon – First Precinct Detective Squad Room

The sergeant's office would be used to question the Zapatas separately. Phineus Fitzroy, the technician, a retired lieutenant and Detective Carlson met when Fitzroy was promoted to lieutenant and Carlson to detective at One Police Plaza. It was a chance meeting, because neither had met the other but their fathers had been partners in the Bronx for a few years. The two radio car partners hugged each other when their eyes met at the promotion ceremony. Father and son met father and son and their relationship developed. Carlson's father died from lung cancer shortly after his promotion. Carlson's mother couldn't deal with the death of her husband and killed herself with a .32 cal. revolver her husband had given her when he was a narcotics detective. Carlson never knew about the revolver. He had taken custody of all of his father's pistols when his father died, except for this one. Carlson quietly took responsibility for his mother's death. He started drinking on the job. One morning he entered the precinct squad room and stood directly in front of Fitzroy, reeking of alcohol. A month later, Carlson left the rehab and had not touched alcohol since. Their friendship grew. "Fitz," as Carlson called him, retired to be a stay-at-home dad. He met a woman thirty years his junior and they married. Three boys later, his wife wanted to return to work and he enjoyed being with his sons. It was a perfect scenario for both. He would do his investigations when his sons were at school, always making sure he had enough time to return to Long Island to pick up his boys when they left school.

The six-foot-two-inch retired lieutenant refused to know anything about the people he would test. He had a basic script along with some questions the detective would always need to be asked. It was Carlson's turn to have his questions asked. Fitzroy made adjustments to his equipment in front of the Zapatas as they were led into their separate rooms. Alan Zapata walked out of his room and over to Carlson.

"Detective, I was wondering if I could sit with my wife until we are ready to be examined. She gets nervous and upset when she has to meet strangers. I am always with her when we go out."

"I guess we could have you stay in the same room with your wife until the technician has completed setting up his equipment. Once the interviews begin, I will need to have the two of you separated at least until the exams are completed."

"I will agree to that. Thank you," Alan said.

Alan walked into the room where Arlene had been sitting. "Feeling better?" he asked.

"Oh my goodness, I am so relaxed," she said.

"Just remember how we practiced. When asked a question, answer it the way we agreed. Take your time. Give yourself time for your body to return to its calm state, then answer the questions. No conflicts. The pills will help you to keep calm but not fog your memory."

"I will do my best but I feel so funny."

"Remember, if the technician asks you if you have taken any drugs this morning, just say no. He can't ask more than that," Alan warned.

"Wish me luck," she said sheepishly.

Alan was relieved that only his wife and the technician would be in the room. If Detective Carlson was in the room, he would know she was on something.

Chief of Detective's Office

Chief Dragonetti sat at his desk, as his secretary, principal, Shirley Brown, handed him a note. He put it on the table and looked up to Brown. She had worked for Dragonetti since he was the commanding officer of the Fifth Precinct fifteen years earlier. Many cops had said that the widowed captain and the divorcee would make a perfect couple but each had their own plans. Brown walked out of her boss's office and slowly closed the door behind her. He didn't read the note until the door was completely closed.

He looked down at the three written lines on the paper. She had developed a terrible handwriting after the first three months working for him. He didn't want anyone to look over his shoulder and look at the contents of any note she had given him. She had practiced bad spelling and mispronunciation of certain words. They worked perfectly together. She wrote terribly and he understood perfectly.

This Zapatas got some juice, Dragonetti thought. He grabbed his jacket and walked to the commissioner's office. He was met by Lieutenant Felix Armstrong, the commanding officer of the police commissioner's office.

"Sorry to bother you, Chief, but the DCPI got a 'heads-up' that the Zapatas were being given a 'lie detector test' without their lawyer present."

Chief Dragonetti stepped around the six foot five three-hundred-pound former Notre Dame star football tackle.

"I'll talk with the commissioner on this."

"But, Chief . . . ," Armstrong began, as he tried to prevent the three-star chief from entering the police commissioner's office.

"Lieu, I'll talk with the commissioner," Chief Dragonetti said and walked through the open door.

Commissioner Tom Kiley, a former track star and life-long athlete sat behind his dark oak desk. His office walls were filled with pictures of him with many public officials. Chief Angelo Dragonetti was unimpressed.

Commissioner Kiley looked up from his desk.

"Chief, you got around my three-hundred-pound star tackle."

Chief Dragonetti stopped and smiled at the commissioner. "I graduated Perdue, we hated those Notre Dame wimps."

"When this is over, we'll have a few, after work, and discuss the good and the bad of both teams. Right now I have this issue I, er, we need to discuss. Angelo, my DCPI, got a 'heads-up' from AP. It seems your detectives ordered the Zapatas to take a lie detector test against their wills. Are they at the First Precinct and do we have to resort to those methods?" Kiley said.

Chief Dragonetti could feel his blood pressure rising. He decided to walk around the commissioner's office for a moment.

"Commissioner, we followed procedure with this case. The sergeant supervising this case came to me with the request to ask the Zapatas if they were willing to take a polygraph test. I ran it by the first dep's office and I got the okay.

"My detective then asked the Zapatas if they would be willing to come into his office and take the test voluntarily, and they agreed. The test is being performed as we speak," Dragonetti said.

"Either the Zapatas are afraid of something or they are looking to score big on their son's loss," Kiley said.

"I haven't received a call that anything went wrong with the interviews," Dragonetti said.

"Well something must have gone wrong because the Zapatas' lawyer wants us to have a meeting with him and the press," Kiley said.

"Commissioner, I will have a meeting with the Zapatas and their lawyer, but the press is out of the question. No press or no meeting."

"Angelo, get back to me by four. I don't want this to go on its own on the *Six O'clock News*."

"Boss, I will have that information for you."

"Angelo, don't let me down."

First Precinct Detective Squad Room
Later That Day

The chief of detectives wore a dark suit, white shirt, and red-and-blue striped tie, as he sat in the creaking swivel chair behind Sergeant Lawrence's desk. Lawrence had rescheduled his tour in order to be present for the administration of the polygraph test. The chief left word at his house that he would be waiting for him. Detective Carlson busied himself by cleaning out the sergeant's coffee pot which hadn't been cleaned in two weeks. "Detective, how did the interview go with the Zapatas?"

"My guy, the technician, and a retired NYPD lieutenant told me the two were completely stoned, and he couldn't tell the truth from blatant bullshit. She had robotic answers."

"Detective, is your guy willing to testify to that?"

"He warned me, if someone lied, the machine could indicate a lie, but there were other factors involved. There was no way he could prove that the answers were in fact a lie."

"Then why pay him?"

"He did what we wanted. We took a chance they would come in sober. I guess we were wrong. Look, even if they came in sober, the hope was the person who was accused of lying would get upset and admit to whatever it was they did or simply take off the straps and walk away. The Zapatas did neither. They sat there for two hours and answered all the questions. The Zapatas took something before the test, and there is absolutely no way we could prove whether they were telling the truth or lying," Carlson said.

"I'll let the commissioner know. He's not going to be happy. I trusted you with your guy and there is no way the Zapatas' attorney will allow another test without his being present. Tell me, how do you know the Zapatas were high?" Dragonetti asked.

"Nine years in Manhattan South Narcotics," Carlson said proudly.

EARLIER THAT DAY
Sergeant Lawrence's Office

Sergeant Lawrence stood at the entrance of his office and watched Phineus Fitzroy set up his equipment. Lawrence had never been present when a polygraph was administered, nor did he know of anyone who had one administered to them, but he was always open to learning something new.

"Fitz, what made you get into this field?" Lawrence asked as he sipped his coffee. Fitzroy continued to work with his equipment for a few moments.

"I love the summer when there is no school. My boys and I have so much fun every day, we go to the beach, hike, and go fishing. My wife is a bit younger than me and she loves her work. The hours are great and I get to pick up my kids at school every afternoon. It will get a little hectic in a couple of years when the oldest gets into middle school. Then murderous after that, because in two years it will be one in high school and one in middle school. The next year, one will be a sophomore in high school, one in middle school, and the last will still be in elementary school. I will be my own 'unmarked' car service," Fitzroy said.

"Can't get the cop talk out of your system," Lawrence said,

"We retire but we never forget. How many businesses out there have *finest* in their corporate logo," Fitzroy said.

"I'm not going anywhere anytime soon," Lawrence said proudly.

"How about I show you how it works?" Fitzroy asked.

"I'm a detective, sergeant. I lie all the time," Lawrence said.

"Do you want to know about this case I got?" Lawrence asked. "I try not to get personal. If I have time when I'm finished, we can talk. I'll need an hour each for the two people."

Carlson wanted to be present when the test was given to the Zapatas, but he got angry when Fitzroy told him he could not be present in the room during the administration of the test.

Alan Zapata wore a button-down shirt with blue jeans and loafers without socks. His hair looked as though it hadn't met with a comb in months. Fitzroy noticed the dirt under Alan Zapata's fingernails when he put the clip on his finger. The underarm odor made the retired lieutenant put the armband around his left arm quickly. He put the tubes across his chest.

He began, "I will ask you a question and I only want a yes or no answer. It is that simple. There is no pass or fail, no red lights going off, you do not get zapped. I will ask you and then your wife the same questions. I will not discuss the results with you. I will give my report to the detectives when I am finished. I will not ask you to explain any of your answers. Detective Carlson may at a later date, but today I am only asking you to give a simple yes or no answer." Fitzroy turned on his machine, walked over, and closed the office door. "Mr. Zapata, do you agree to answer all the questions I may ask you in a fair and honest manner?"

"I will," Alan said meekly.

"Yes or no only, please."

"Sorry."

The testing lasted about an hour and ten minutes as Alan needed some time to remember. Arlene flew through the process in fifty minutes which surprised even Fitzroy.

Once he was given permission to enter the room, Alan Zapata raced in to hug his wife. He whispered, "How did you do?"

She smiled and said, "I'm hungry, let's have lunch."

They walked out of the First Precinct station house into the flow of the exiting traffic of the Holland Tunnel. The car horns were blaring, most of the office workers were in their buildings already. The beat-up cars, or the ones with the missing hub caps, were usually the junkies from Bayonne looking to get high and they were late and getting itchy. Alan and Arlene made their way through the traffic back to their apartment.

Detective Joseph followed a block back. He would report back to Carlson and Lawrence.

15

Remembering Joyce's House

Joyce sat in his gold crushed velvet recliner as he waited for the commercials to end, he watched the *Six O'clock News*. He finished adjusting the aluminum fins on the antennae wings as Elizabeth coached him. Their house was three houses away from the water's edge of Great Kills Harbor. The original view of the water and walks on the beach lasted six months before development crowded the shoreline. Every hurricane season, he would spend time watching the shoreline rise and recede. Their house was a small duplex but attached to some great neighbors. Frank was a CIA agent who spent long trips away. Casey, his wife, and Elizabeth became close friends. Frank never talked about his work, Joyce couldn't refrain from bragging.

Joyce pushed the footrest down and stepped over to the TV set to increase the volume and make a minor adjustment to the color mix of the TV. The reporter began, "This just in, two New York assemblymen have launched an investigation into the NYPD's accusation that Alan and Arlene Zapata were involved with the disappearance of their son, Nate."

"Are they shitting me, the detectives probably asked the parents to submit to a polygraph test to clear them," Joyce said.

"Honey, do you really believe that the parents of that little boy killed their son?" Elizabeth asked.

"I question the timing," Joyce mumbled.

"What are you going to do about it?" she asked.

"Not sure, I'm a cop, just a uniformed cop on patrol. Who is going to listen to me when they have all these powerful detectives working the case?"

"How much does it matter that the two assemblymen came out in support of the Zapatas and questioned the NYPD?" she asked.

"Honey, you have to understand how One Police Plaza works. It's like a bee honeycomb. The PC is the queen bee and the rest of the people are the worker bees. If the PC sneezes, all the workers stop what they are doing and say, 'Bless you,' collectively, including the people working in the basement."

"That's so funny," Elizabeth said.

"Not if you're working there, and if you decide to go out and get a cup of coffee from a local coffee shop, you are questioned by at least seven people as to why you are going outside. It is like they fear you are going to tell the newspapers that they ran out of toilet paper in the men's bathroom again," Joyce said.

"Why would anyone want to work there in the first place?"

"Being up the commissioner's ass or one of his chiefs' is a great way of getting promoted. That includes the detectives, sergeants, and lieutenants," Joyce said.

"Bob, tell me the truth, would you work there, if it meant a promotion?"

"It's not for me. The test results for the sergeants' exam will be finalized next week. I like the streets way too much, and besides, I like my balls just the way they are, always ready for you."

"Upstairs, future sergeant, let's give our daughter a brother or sister to play ball with."

I guess I'll miss the Mets tonight, Joyce thought.

Later

Joyce listened for his daughter's middle-of-the-night call for a bottle. He was interrupted when Elizabeth stood in the doorway, drying her hair, naked.

"You haven't done that in a while."

"What, dry my hair?"

"No, it's the way you stand naked in the doorway. I can't tell you the last time you did that."

Elizabeth stood with her long legs straddling the doorway threshold. Her left hand was holding the towel and her right hand was on her hip. "That's your 'That was good, now let's do it again' stance, and you have not done that in a while," he said.

"Two years ago, September twelfth," she said.

Joyce had finished his last set of midnights. It was a Saturday morning. She thought he made a collar, because he always came straight home after a midnight tour. She waited for a call, but there was none, and since a priest and two uniformed cops hadn't knocked at the front door, she knew he was still alive. She decided to do a ten-mile run. She finished it easily and opened the front door, still no sign of her husband. She wasn't going to call the desk sergeant to ask the sergeant where her husband was, he could never live that down, she decided to take a shower. She thought she heard a noise, she pushed the shower curtain to the side. There stood a man, naked as she was, standing by her bathroom door. Her heart began to beat faster. "Well, it's about time you came home," she said as her husband approached her and pushed her back into the shower and turned on the water. She held him but wanted to scream at him for not calling her.

He never told her about the upcoming sergeant's test. She was the student who studied all the time. He did all his studying at court. There was so much downtime, the only alternative was to go with the guys to the "Recess Bar" for a couple. He decided he'd rather be a sergeant than a drunk.

He couldn't take the midnight off the night before the test to sleep, because the senior cops had already depleted the platoon for the night. His biggest fear was that he would make a collar and miss the test entirely. He had little time to stand in line for one of the telephones to become free at the station house. He had hoped that there would be some phone booths at the high school where he was scheduled to take the test. He parked his car illegally, because of time, and raced into Lincoln High School. There was a single pay phone in the lobby of the school and a line of twenty or so cops trying to call home.

Later in the afternoon, he again wanted to call Elizabeth but he could not find an unoccupied pay phone. He knew he was going to catch hell from his wife. He never remembered driving to his house on Staten Island from the high school in Brooklyn. He saw her running shoes by the front door and heard the water running in the upstairs bathroom. Liz always showered after she did her run. Though they were married for a long time, they always ran alone. He decided to do something different. He removed his clothes and left himself at her mercy. Nine months Jennifer was born.

16

Finders Keepers Saint John's Cemetery, Trenton, New Jersey

Present Day

Saint John's Catholic Cemetery was established in the early to mid-1810s, at best guess. The original Saint John's Church on Laylor Street, was built in 1814. It burned down and another replacement church was planned, but the location was moved to Center Street in 1848, which was the same year Joyce's great, great grand-father built his house next to the church. That church burned down in the 1880s on the spot where the present brick structure sits today. Joyce's parents passed away in the early and mid-1990s. His father started to do a family history, or a genealogy trace of his relatives, but lung cancer put a halt to that. In his father's honor, Joyce resumed the journey. He and Elizabeth researched both their family histories which went back over four hundred years. He knew the inside and out of each cemetery in many states. He could tell the workers where to find hidden notes and documents on people buried in some very secular cemeteries. He had the time now, their children were married, and Bob Joyce and Elizabeth had grandchildren to tend to on occasion. He loved the research and the unexpected discoveries. One thing always sat at the back of his mind, all throughout his police days, the investigation of Nate Zapata had gone frozen, not just cold, it went frozen, until Fausto Munoz made his statement to his cousin.

He was now a licensed private investigator and loved to hand out his card. It seemed that a private investigator was held to a higher regard than a retired police lieutenant, though the shield and retired ID did open more doors.

Joyce and Elizabeth walked through the small cemetery, but in separate "sections."

"Honey, it's over here," Joyce called out.

"It's about time. We've been through a hundred to a hundred and fifty cemeteries since we started our family's ancestry. Why is it that my family's graves were so easy to find? Your family is buried all over the place, for God's sake."

"Blame me for my great-grandparents' decision on their burial location."

"It's not that, it's just that I have no interest in looking for your great-great-great-great-uncle Peter who may have fought in the Civil War."

Joyce looked at the dates on the gravestone; he mumbled to himself, "That was Charles Carol and it was the Revolutionary War."

"I'm putting you on notice, this is my last cemetery visit for your family. Take someone else, how about your old partner Carol Bini, she is a grandmother and has the time."

"Let's go to dinner and have a glass of wine or two and talk this over. I might just take you up on your offer."

"Fine."

17

Atlantic City

The ride from Saint John's Cemetery in Trenton to Atlantic City was quiet for the couple. Joyce enjoyed riding with the top down on his Mustang Convertible, but a slight rain had fallen and forced him to pull to the side of the road and put up the top.

"You wished that on me, didn't you?" Joyce said and pulled back into traffic.

"This is your 'pick-up' car. My hair always goes in forty-nine different directions at once, when I sit in this seat, or rather anywhere in this car," she said.

"Hey, the only other place you could sit in the car and have your hair blow around is the driver's seat and you know I don't want you to drive Anni."

"Anni, Anni, Anni, all I hear is that you and the car drove here and there. It's a car, not a girlfriend," Elizabeth said.

"You need a drink," Joyce said.

"You're damn right I need a drink," she said angrily.

"To the Irish Pub, before we lose all our money," Joyce said.

"I'm sorry, but all these cemetery visits get me on edge. Looking at your great-great-grandfather's name and date of death, on his tombstone, your great-grandfather's grave without a headstone, your grandfather and father's headstone in Holy Cross Cemetery. It seems that all we think about is death and burials," she said.

"I don't know why I ever convinced you to start looking for your family and then my family ancestry, but I am glad I did," Joyce said as he drove along 195 to the Garden State Parkway.

"Something is calling me to find these graves, look at what happened when we discovered my father's mother's parents and her brother and sister's grave."

"See stop right there, you say that so easily to me, but to someone who hasn't spent all these days, months, and years searching, through state archives, church and cemetery records, what you just said would have to be written on a sheet of paper with a diagram for them to understand."

"I know that I take the information I have nonchalantly, but I have broken through that wall, the wall the people operating the cemeteries have put up. They make a deceased person's relatives pay for information about their long-gone or, to be blunt, dead relatives. They give you a teaser and ask you for one relative's name. You give them a relative that is positively buried at the cemetery, because it is on the death certificate," Joyce said.

Elizabeth was now interested. "Yet not all death certificates are correct when it comes to burial locations. Relatives change their minds at the last minute but forget to tell the undertaker or a fifty-dollar bill relaxes the memory of the funeral director," she said.

"The grave opening and closings are always on the grave card. The cemetery people take you through this long-drawn-out process to find out who else is in the grave with your relative. They do a dog and pony show about how they get the recorded information from micro film, sheets and sheets of clear plastic with dead people's names and where they are buried. They are the mystery family, people who may be distant cousins, so you pay the ridiculous fee. You get a letter in the mail with all the names in the grave with your relative. You don't recognize the names, and of course, all you get are names and/or possibly dates of internments. Then it is back to vital records of the state and reinvestigate your relative's death and the people who may be on the certificate. It is there you see that they died in a public hospital of a rare or communicable disease. Your relative had been quarantined because of the disease. Remember my great-uncle, my grandfather's brother who we found buried in Calvary Cemetery. So I asked who owned the grave, the man behind the counter, after a ten-minute hide-and-seek with his records, looked at a small card and said, 'He purchased his grave in 1860.'

I shook my head slowly, smiled, and said, "That's very interesting since my great-uncle wasn't born until 1878."

"I always wondered about that, but I didn't want to say anything," Elizabeth said.

"The Irish were all guilty of putting up their grave plots in a poker game. Some had six to eight plots signed over to them after a long night of card playing," he said.

"Is it against the law to gamble away a grave plot?" she asked.

"Not really, but the hospital people usually forced the owner of the certificate to allow them to use the remaining spaces in the grave to burry other 'inmates' as they were called in the census. The current plot owner had the first choice of the people he wanted to lay with for the remainder of eternity and had to sign off on the certificate so he couldn't use it to bet with again."

"I see nothing wrong with that," Elizabeth said.

"Absolutely nothing wrong with it except when they charge someone hundreds of dollars to look at a card and have someone type in the names on a piece of paper. The names are not the long-lost family of your deceased relative, just some gambling friends of your relative. A nice little scheme to make money," he said.

"I am now so mad, I really need a drink.

Joyce made the sharp right off of the Garden State Parkway onto the Atlantic Expressway. Joyce and Elizabeth called out the names on the billboards. "Oh my god, are they still alive?" Elizabeth said.

"I don't know about them, but some of them should retire or at least dye their hair, what hair still remain on the sides of their heads," Joyce said.

He turned left at the chariots and drove for another six blocks and parked in the open field. Joyce put his parking permit on the dashboard. The wind off the ocean blew Elizabeth's hair in forty-nine different directions as she held her balance against the wind. The wood door creaked as Joyce pulled on it against the onslaught of the easterly wind off the nearby ocean. A customer pushed on the door as he tried to exit, making Joyce's door opening seem effortlessly. The man stumbled into Joyce's chest. He was obviously intoxicated. He held his right index finger to his mouth. "My wife is in the casino and doesn't know I'm here," the very intoxicated man said.

A voice over Joyce's shoulder, "Mr. Godfrey, it's me Paul, the car is over here. The misses went to bed three hours ago. I guess you want to go back to the room?" the chauffeur said.

"Hell no, the bitch is fast asleep and will never know what time I came back," he whispered to Joyce.

Joyce stood the man up against the wall for a moment as the chauffeur waited. "Mr. Godfrey, I am Lieutenant Hymie Gnatz of the Atlantic City Police Department, if you go back inside, I will have to place you under arrest. Now I will help you over to your car and your driver will take you back to your room. I have placed a GPS device under your car, so I will know when you get back to your hotel," Joyce said.

The man tried to take a step back, but Joyce held his arms to keep him from falling down. He caught his balance. "Lieutenant, do you know who I am?" he said proudly.

"Now, Bob, don't say it," Elizabeth remarked.

Joyce grabbed the man by the collar of his suit jacket and his belt and lifted him off the ground. "Sir, this way," the chauffeur said. Joyce gently led the man into the wide backseat of the limousine. Mr. Godfrey immediately fell fast asleep on the backseat.

The chauffeur held out his hand to shake Joyce's hand. Joyce noticed the folded currency. His instinct was to refuse, but now he didn't give a crap. He held out his hand and the chauffeur slid the currency into Joyce's palm. Joyce smiled and slid the money into his pocket and walked into the secluded Irish restaurant with Elizabeth.

The Irish rebel music played softly over the well-hidden ceiling speakers. They slowly walked through the souvenir shop. They both loved to look at the Irish-themed items for sale.

"When he gets bigger, I'm going to get our grandson one of those 'Tams' to wear for St. Patrick's Day."

"Remember we also have a granddaughter and another one on the way," Elizabeth said coldly.

"That's your job. I'll teach our grandson how to shoot, you can teach our granddaughters how to knit.'

"Knit, I don't know how to knit," Elizabeth said as the waitress approached.

"Sit anywhere you'd like," the waitress said and walked off.

"Lead the way," Joyce said with a smile.

Elizabeth picked a table in the far corner of the restaurant. She allowed her husband to sit with his back against the wall. It was a cop's favorite table position, with his/her back against a wall. They talked about her great-grandfather's missing stone. His grave cost seven dollars when he died. He had no money for a stone to mark his final resting spot. Joyce slid his hand into his pocket and removed the money the chauffeur had given him. Three one-hundred-dollar bills slid out of his pocket. He closed his hand and returned the bills to the bottom of his pocket. The waitress took their drink orders and walked away. Elizabeth excused herself. Joyce was alone, he was happy to have the time alone to think.

Two men in their middle to late thirties, cop looking, sat at the table next to Joyce's table. Joyce immediately saw the gold shield and a Glock 9mm on the man's left side. The second man excused himself and Joyce and the stranger were alone.

"I see you're a lefty shooter," Joyce said softly as he showed his NYPD lieutenant's shield to the cop. "NYPD, retired lieutenant, Bob Joyce."

"Detective Gordon Clark, Camden PD, down here on a warrant investigation."

"My wife, Elizabeth, and I have been doing some ancestry over in Trenton and decided to make a night of it down here," Joyce said.

"It's nice to be retired," Clark said as Elizabeth returned.

"He's retired but he hasn't stopped investigating," Elizabeth said as she sat next to her husband.

"Detective Clark, meet my wife, Elizabeth," Joyce said. Elizabeth put out her hand and then noticed his weapon. "Don't worry, honey, he's from Camden PD, he can carry down here," Joyce said.

"My first name is Gordon, ma'am."

"Elizabeth Joyce," she said as she held out her hand.

The waitress brought Elizabeth a gin and tonic and her husband a beer. "I'd offer to buy you and your partner a beer but drinking on the job is not in my book," Joyce said.

"Ginger ale and a Diet Coke are our choice of drink," Clark said.

"Hey, Jim Walsh, nice to meet you, folks," Walsh said as he sat at his table.

"Jim, this is Elizabeth and Bob Joyce. He is retired from the NYPD," Gordon said.

"Hey, we worked with some of your guys on that Nate Zapata case, because Fausto Munoz lived in our town."

"You said Nate Zapata, right?" Elizabeth said.

"Yeah, we worked with your guys for almost two years, helping them with their investigation," Walsh continued.

Elizabeth turned to her husband and then to the detectives. “He’ll be right over.”

Joyce got up from their table, took a long sip of the beer, and placed it back on the table and walked over to their table and grabbed a chair.

“I was a cop on the night the little boy went missing. We were mobilized to his building that night. I got to search his apartment house and a bunch of the surrounding buildings. There are just too many pieces to this puzzle that just don’t fit. His second trial began two weeks ago, it may be a couple of months until the jury gets to vote.”

Joyce looked at both men. “Do you think Munoz is guilty?”

Gordon Clark looked over to his partner then returned his attention to Joyce. “Based on what they told us, we both don’t believe he did it.”

“Did they tell you that the boy’s mother originally said she followed her son to the school bus stop that morning, then changed her story to putting herself back across the street, then at the steps to her building, and just the other day, she suddenly remembered that she was in her apartment and wished her son a good-bye and he walked out the door to the apartment? Joyce asked.

Clark turned to his partner with a very surprised expression. “No,” he responded quietly.

“Did they tell you that the boy should have been home at three in the afternoon but the mother didn’t call the precinct until about six, almost three hours later?”

“No,” Clark repeated.

Joyce continued about his building search and the mother’s demeanor when he entered the hallway. He ended with the statement from the junkie building super.

Both detectives looked down at their plates and pushed their food to the center of the table.

"There is a lot more that has not been entered into evidence, yet they somehow believe the boy's mother's statement after she changed her story six times. I'm sorry to put this all on you, guys. I have been walking around with this information since that night. No one wants to listen."

Joyce slid his business card with his e-mail and cell phone number on it to each of the detectives. "I'll leave you guys alone, my food is getting cold as it always does once I start talking about the case."

"Thank you for that information, Lieutenant, I want the guys in the office to hear what you said about Munoz's innocence, because that was the general consensus in the office," Clark said.

The Casino

Joyce and Elizabeth went to their favorite casino, he played blackjack and she liked the slots. It was getting late, so they decided to only spend an hour gambling. They kissed and wished each other good luck and went their separate ways. Elizabeth went to her favorite machine which was surprisingly vacant. He walked over to the tables. One table was occupied with seven gamblers, the other had only two at the table, it was then Joyce noticed the minimum bet had been changed from ten dollars to twenty-five dollars and the maximum bet was now ten thousand dollars. He put his three-hundred-dollar tip on the table along with his card and pointed to the single one-hundred-dollar bill on the table. "I want three quarters and five nickels, the other two leave at one-hundred-dollar chips."

Joyce saw the yellow card on the table and kept his chips in his hand until the dealer finished shuffling the deck. The automatic shuffling machine was not working. It took a minute for the dealer to shuffle the five or so decks of cards. Joyce didn't mind. He was playing with someone else's money. The dealer was ready. Joyce took one of the five-dollar chips and put it on the lucky lady circle. He put a twenty-five-dollar chip as his bet. The dealer slid the first set of cards. Joyce had a queen of hearts. He smiled. Two aces went to the two other betters and the dealer had a ten of spades.

"Wouldn't it be interesting if you got the second queen of hearts and I got an ace," the Pacific Island dealer said with a thick accent.

Joyce's body was racing. His maximum personal bet was always two five-dollar chips and nothing higher. A twenty-five-dollar bet was far beyond anything Joyce had ever offered as a bet. The dealer began to slide the cards out of the chute. The player to his right got a queen of hearts to make a blackjack, he was happy. "Could I buy his card for a fee?" Joyce said jokingly. The Pacific Island dealer said nothing but did smile. He drew Joyce's second card; it was also a queen of hearts. Joyce's heart kept its rhythmic beat, he already won a thousand dollars on his bet, but if the dealer got blackjack, he would win five thousand dollars. The third person at the table got a queen of diamonds. Blackjack was the deal of the day. The dealer slid his second card under his lead card. He pulled it to his viewer and looked. "Insurance anyone or even money," he said with a broad smile on his face. Joyce didn't take the offer. The dealer turned over his down card, he had an ace. The two other players roared approval even though they only got a push on their blackjacks, Joyce won five thousand dollars. The dealer moved his hands away from all the cards and called his "pit boss" over for approval. The fifty-something supervisor looked at Joyce's bet and the cards, confirmed it with the cameras, and Joyce was given ten, five-hundred-dollar chips. He scooped up the chips and walked away from the table. He stopped and went back to the table and tossed a one-hundred-dollar chip to the dealer. The dealer tapped the metal box to his left and entered the chip through the slot and pushed it down. Joyce walked over to the adjoining table and stopped. The table's dealer had his decks splayed on the table and Joyce waited for the dealer to shuffle the eight decks of playing cards. The minimum bet was ten dollars and the maximum was now a thousand dollars. He ordered a glass of Pinot Gregio wine, he felt lucky. He decided to max out his bet to the table limit. He was now betting a thousand dollars. He knew if Elizabeth had seen his bet, she would have been very angry. He was glad she was at her favorite slot machine, out of sight of him as he played. Joyce was wondering when he would awaken from this dream. His first card was a ten, the player to his right got a three, and the one to his left a seven. The dealer showed a four. The dealer slowly slid the card out of the slide and turned it to himself before displaying it to Joyce and the other players. It was an ace of diamonds, Joyce had black jack.

His mind said to move but his body wanted to stay. He held the four five-hundred-dollar chips in his hand which remained inside his pants pocket. He wanted to bet another thousand but pulled out a twenty-five-dollar chip and put it on the table. His first two cards were a nine and a duce, he had eleven, the dealer had a six showing. All reasoning in his brain said for him to double down. He took a second twenty-five-dollar chip and put it next to his original bet and waited. The dealer slowly slid the card from the chute, Joyce got a three and the dealer put it sideways, signaling only one card was allowed. The two other betters had a total of eighteen and twenty collectively. "His down card is going to be a five," Joyce said. The dealer turned over his down card, it was a jack of spades. He had to take another card. The Asian men to either side of him began shouting, "Monkey, monkey, monkey." The dealer slid out his third card, it was a five. His hand won. The pit boss walked over to the sign and changed the minimum bet to one hundred dollars and a maximum of ten thousand dollars. Joyce wanted to bet all his money but played carefully as he finished his glass of Pinot Gregio. He ordered a second glass, the pit boss immediately signaled for the waitress.

Elizabeth was always the conservative and careful bettor. She loved playing the penny slots while her husband played his table games. Her favorite slot machine was centrally located in the smoking section of the casino. She looked at her watch. If he was winning, she would have to go look for him. If he was losing, he would return to her area of slots and play the penny slots alongside of her. Her balance went to empty. She was disappointed but she had had enough of the smoke. She turned to see her husband holding a five-dollar bill out to insert into a machine next to her machine. He handed her a five-dollar bill and a gin and tonic.

"How did you do?" she asked.

“I was up, but they take it right back,” he said. They played for a while. Joyce looked at his cell phone before ordering another Pinot Gregio.

“This will be our first time doing an overnighter without a change of clothes, could we leave early, like right after breakfast?” he asked.

“Sure, something important on your phone?” she asked.

“That’s the problem, I’m not getting anything. I think my cell phone is acting crazily again.”

“You can use my phone,” she said innocently.

“Let’s get up early. I’ll drive back home and then I can go for a run,” he said.

“I just need to go to the car first, I think I left my lipstick on my seat. You go to the room and shower, I’ll meet you there,” she said.

Twenty Minutes Later

Joyce opened the door to the bathroom as Elizabeth opened the door to their room. She was carrying a black leather bag he had given her years earlier. He had a towel wrapped around his waist as he towel-dried his hair.

“Where did you get that?” he asked.

“It’s sort of like my ‘to-go’ bag, you know in case of emergencies, you gave it to me for an anniversary present,” she said innocently.

“Only for you,” he asked and walked back into the bathroom.

“No, I have your personal stuff, shaving cream, deodorant, and other stuff.”

"Other stuff like what?" he asked.

"A T-shirt, boxers, jammie bottoms, socks, toothbrush and paste, the usual stuff you and I need for an overnight," she said.

"We never planned for an overnight, did we?" he asked.

"We have it, so if you have 'em, wear 'em," she said. It was then she noticed the ice bucket with the tall stem to a bottle of champagne. "Where did that come from?" she asked.

"I kind of won a bit," he said sheepishly.

"How much did you kind of win?" she asked.

Joyce walked over to the bucket and picked up the bottle of champagne and removed the gold foil and the wire which secured the cork. He wrapped a towel around the cork stopper and pulled it out of the bottle gently. There was a low pop but no spillage..

"Can you get the two glasses from next to the bucket, I'll pour."

It was then she noticed his three stacks of poker chips. "How much did you win?"

"Give me the glasses and then count them." He poured the champagne into the glasses as she moved the chips.

She turned around and smiled. "One glass and then we celebrate, and then we get drunk," she said. He handed her a glass. She drank it down in one gulp, he followed. She looked at his towel. Then she reached over and pulled it off him. Three seconds later, her clothes were on the floor.

Early the Next Morning

Joyce sat at the computer table, trying to put the chips in a single tall column. The champagne bottle was empty, Elizabeth still had no idea how much money her husband had won the night before. He counted the chips eight times. He had shaven and he brushed his teeth, he was ready to rush down to the cashier's window. He waited for a moment. He had won $27,500 in less than forty-five minutes earlier that night. He looked at his watch and grabbed half the chips and put the remainder into the room safe.

He wrote a note, "I'll be back in a minute." He put it on the wall over the toilet. He took the elevator and went to the casino floor. It was almost empty, he walked quickly to the cashier's window, smiled, and slid ten five-hundred-dollar chips to her. She was tired and looked at her watch, her shift was almost over. She slid them out so the camera could see the chips. She counted out the fifty one-hundred-dollar bills and stacked them. She looked out over the successful gambler and slid them to him. Joyce reached in under the gate and grabbed the bills. He folded them and slid them into his pocket. He looked around and walked away momentarily as the shifts changed. He repeated the process with the relief. Later it would be Elizabeth's turn at the window.

Garden State Parkway
Inside Joyce's Mustang

"Tell me again how you were able to pull yourself away from the table?" Elizabeth asked.

"I wanted to stay and make thirty thousand but I suddenly remembered a friend of mine, a cop, he told me he went to AC with five hundred dollars and was on the blackjack table, just like I was, and he was up forty-five hundred dollars and wanted to make it an even five thousand. Not only did he lose the forty-five hundred but the original five hundred dollars he went there with. That has always stayed with me. There was this older black woman, a little plain, silver hair, a touch of makeup, and she wore an old-fashioned below-the-knee-length dress, black with white dots. I have a picture of my grandmother in a dress like that," he said.

"It's in your office, I've seen it."

"There came a point where I couldn't lose a hand, the cards were with me and I ordered another glass of wine. When it came, she went to say something and accidentally knocked it over. The pit boss immediately called for the waitress to get me another glass. The black woman apologized. The pit boss grabbed a handful of paper towels and wiped up the wine. Most of it rolled off the side of the table, away from where the cards were to go. I turned to her and touched her arm and said, 'No need to apologize for something you did intentionally.'

"'I have been coming down here for way too many years, it is not something to be proud of. I was so happy for you when you kept winning. Did you notice how many times they changed dealers?' she said.

"'No, I didn't,' I said.

"'It's a superstition down here. Remove the player's lucky dealer and you remove his luck, but you kept winning. Did you see how quickly they had the waitress go and replace the glass I knocked over?' she said.

"'No. I didn't.'

"'You were too busy enjoying your winnings to see the reinforcements come in. The two additional gamblers that sat at the table with us were shills for the casino. They were trying to break your luck, and it didn't work. Listen, I'm a few years older than you, I have seen men come down here with their down payments on a house and lose all of it playing blackjack. They would cry and beg for more money to win back their losings. It never happened for them. They would have to go back to their wives and tell them they had lost the money. I can't tell you how many men I have seen come down here with their spouses and, years later, start coming down alone and disheveled,' she said. 'I bet some women are the same way,' I said.

"'Have you ever sat alone at a slot machine away from your wife and a woman out of the blue sits down next to you and asks you if you are staying overnight?' she said.

"'Yeah, I remember a time when a woman approached me and asked me that. I told her I was, but that I would have to ask my wife if she would be interested in a threesome.'

"'Don't you think that could have been an elaborate scam?' the woman said. She warned me about the evils of the casinos as though I were a twenty-one-year-old playing at the table for the first time."

Joyce smiled as he continued to drive. He was doing seventy-nine miles an hour.

"Elizabeth, let's look at this like I look at the Nate Zapata case."

Elizabeth turned to look out her window. "Why does everything have to relate to the Nate Zapata case?" she said.

"I want to throw this out there, you have already listened to the circumstantial evidence of the Nate case. Last night could have been a scam or a set up for a robbery. We come down to AC on a whim, we decide to go eat at the Irish pub instead of gambling first. I bump into a very rich, drunk man as I open the door. I help him to his car and his chauffeur gives me a three-hundred-dollar tip. We meet two Camden County detectives who just happen to be down at AC on a warrant investigation. I easily saw their shields and weapons. I introduced myself and showed them my shield. They introduced themselves and mention why they were in Atlantic City. They mentioned the Zapata case and you volunteer me. I chatted with them. We go to the casino and I have three hundred dollars, thanks to the drunk millionaire's generous chauffeur. I go to a table that is way out of my limits and I bet the free money and win. I continue to win at different tables and finally end up next to an African American gambler. She talks me down from gambling and I go back to our room with over twenty-seven thousand dollars in casino chips. I won and we have the money. If you add up all the possibilities and put them into a basket without my reasoning, yeah, it could have been a setup but it didn't happen. The chauffeur was a chauffeur, and that was it. The changing of the dealers didn't affect my winning. Adding two additional players at my table did nothing.

"Arlene Zapata stated that Nate left to go to school that morning as they had agreed. She said she allowed Nate to leave the apartment alone and walk to his school bus stop alone. Someone must have mentioned to her that letting her son go to the bus stop alone was one of the dumbest things a mother could allow her son to do.

She changed her story. The second version was that she said she followed her son as he walked to the bus stop and how he even stopped at the corner and waited for the traffic light to turn green before crossing. She stated she waited across the street and watched her son get on the school bus. Carol and I proved that her statement that she saw her son get on his yellow school bus was a physical impossibility. Though she could have seen him walk to the school bus stop, seeing him get on the bus could not have happened as the school bus would have blocked her view of her son actually getting on the bus. The other parents of the children who were with their children, at the bus-stop remember not seeing Nate that morning being at the bus stop alone or getting on the bus stop. Some had told the detectives that they would have been surprised to see Nate at the bus stop alone. That version of the story didn't hold water so she changed her version placing herself mid-block and watching her son get on the school bus, but the parent's version remains the same, Nate never showed up at the bus stop. That version did not bode well, so she said at the first trial, while she was on the witness stand, that she watched Nate from the steps of their apartment house and then she testified she climbed out onto their fire-escape and watched him make his way to the bus-stop. She and her husband both posed for photographers as they stood on the fire escape and pretended, as she did that morning, to watch their son go to the bus stop. Yet no one has picked up on these not so subtle changes. The last and most recent was last week where she stated under oath at the second trial of Fausto Munoz that she said good-by to her son from inside the apartment and wished him well. Yet the parents of the other students at Nate's school bus stop stated they never saw Nate at the bus-stop nor did he get on the bus. Still everyone is silent on this matter, including Fausto's defense attorney. Why? Arlene's statements have changed six times and no one questions that issue, not even Fausto's defense attorney. Why?" "Is the father letting his wife change her story to show she is lying," Elizabeth said. "Good point."

An unmarked NJ State trooper car pulled behind Joyce, he was speeding. He was doing ninety-two. Joyce knew the trooper would see the small Blue Lives Matter sticker under the NY State insignia on his rear license plate. The unmarked state trooper car sped into the middle lane and sped ahead to catch a speeder, Joyce resumed. He was now doing only eighty-five miles an hour.

Oh yeah, one reporter did write that the prosecutor dismissed Arlene's remembrance of where she actually walked to, stood, and watched her son, was just a lapse of memory."

"Oh really, it seems that she is the only one with the bad memory," Joyce said.

"I know exactly where I was, what I was doing, and what I was wearing when I got the call to put on the television to see that an airplane had crashed into one of the towers of the World Trade Center on 9/11. I certainly would know where I was and what I was doing when and if my son failed to come home from school," Elizabeth said coldly.

Elizabeth shifted her position, something she had never done in his car ever. She was now looking directly at her husband. "You told me and you always said that you told your cops, if you tell the truth, you never have to remember anything."

"Fausto worked at the bodega and he said he had free access to the basement, the diamond steel access gates were kept open during the morning rush. That didn't happen. The gates were closed and locked each and every time someone had to go to the basement and that person was watched by the store owner. Then Fausto said he carried Nate's sixty-pound body out of the basement in a thirty-five-gallon black plastic trash bag. There is no way the owner would have allowed him to carry out such a large bulging bag and simply walk away. That wouldn't have happened. Then Fausto said he put the bag on some steps, a block or two away from the store, on his way home from work. Nope, that didn't happen. The commercial trash is always picked up during the night. That way the private carting service can get around the streets of Manhattan easily. It would be almost impossible to try and complete their collection route during a normal business day. Many of the bodega owners took the one or two bags of paper trash home with them and put it out with their regular household trash."

"Remember when we moved into our second house and Bobby put a large sugar gumball in his closet, we had a trail of carpenter ants breakdancing across our carpet into his room and then back out. You went crazy and had me hire an exterminator to get rid of them, but remember they never altered their path to and from their food, even though we stood over them. The junkies in the seventies did the same. They came from Bayonne to the lower east side, passing through SoHo, to get their heroin. They always looked down for loose change or anything that may fall out of someone's pant's pocket. They would notice a Hispanic teen carrying a large plastic bag who suddenly dropped it on some building steps. They, the junkies, would suspect the teen was carrying proceeds to a burglary and may have seen a cop, parole or probation officer in the distance and tossed away the evidence. It would be their turn at the goodies. They would have found Nate but there was no bag, no evidence, no Nate, nothing."

"Don't they pay a monthly fee?" Elizabeth asked.

"Not really. Large grocery stores and restaurants, yes, they have a lot of heavy trash that needs to be picked up every night. Small stores like bodegas are a little different. NYC Sanitation Department requires all business owners to have a sticker displayed in their store's front window, usually by the front door at the bottom of the window, designating the carting company that picks up their trash. Remember my friend Martha who had a beauty parlor on Third Avenue? Well, one day she complained to me when a sanitation cop gave her a ticket for no sticker displayed in her store's front window. She wanted me to fix the ticket. She pleaded with the cop, saying she only had a small bag of trash at the end of the day. He countered by saying the City imposed a regulation for such that reason, because many of the small store owners were taking their business trash and putting it into the street corner receptacles to avoid having to have to pay a standard fee for a little bag of trash. Two weeks later, I was walking my foot post and there was Martha standing outside her beauty parlor with a big smile on her face. I knew she was up to something.

"'I got my sticker on my window, but I don't have to pay for a small bag of trash. I paid fifty dollars for the sticker and that's all I needed to avoid a ticket,' she said to me proudly," Joyce said.

Joyce looked at his fuel gauge and pulled into the rest area for gas. “Fill it regular,” Joyce said and it would be the first time in a very long time that he would not be using his credit card to pay for the gas. He turned back to Elizabeth. “Any room for another cup of coffee?”

“Sure, you’re the big spender,” she joked.

Joyce walked to the food center and remembered when the only thing in a gas station was an old Coca-Cola dispensing machine, and the bottle of soda was ten cents.

He walked over to the self-service counter and made two medium-size cups of coffee. He used a long stirrer for the coffees and put the lids on. He looked around for a trash bin. “Hey, where do I put this?” Joyce said as he held up the long plastic straw.

“In the cup next to the sugar,” the woman behind the counter said in broken English.

A man walked out of the room next to her. “That’s the first time anyone has asked where the trash can was for the stirrer,” the man said.

“How long have you owned this franchise?” Joyce asked.

“Too long. Looking to buy one?” he said

“No really, how long have you owned it?” Joyce asked again.

“Three years.”

Joyce looked around the store, it had seven refrigerators to keep the bottles of soda and water cold. Racks of chips and pretzels. “Say, I’ve noticed the large container outside for the trash. Does this store generate that much trash?”

“Most of the trash comes from you motorists who decide to do their monthly car cleaning when they come and fill up. My trash is a single bag, mostly coffee grinds, tea bags, empty milk containers. My customers come in here and take everything with them, until they have to fill up again and then my cups and bottles go into the next guy's trash. The owners want the waste bins as a service to the highways and the environment and of course the customers."

Joyce walked over to Elizabeth's side of the car and handed her the cups of coffee. He looked at the cost of the gas and turned to the very displeased gas attendant. He handed the attendant a fifty-dollar bill and said, "Keep the change." The mid-forties-something man now had a broad smile on his face.

Joyce climbed into the Mustang, reset the miles per gallon gauge out of habit. It was back to talking about Nate Zapata. Joyce didn't start right away, he thought about when he worked in the luncheonette on the corner by the Beverly Theatre in Brooklyn. He worked there mostly in the summertime, and he helped out during the holidays. He learned to flip eggs, make chocolate egg creams, Lime Rickeys, Vanilla Cokes, ice cream floats, banana splits, tuna, egg and chicken salads were easy to make as it only required him to scoop out the salad and put it on the customer's choice of bread and spread. He always remembered to have the large lump in the middle as he cut the bread. It always looked as though the customer was getting a thick overstuffed sandwich. He could work six coffees at a time, medium, light, dark, there was no decaf or skim, 1% or 2%, it was whole milk only, and only one size coffee cup, and it was a twelve ounce cup. He could put together a hundred and fifty Sunday daily newspapers in ten minutes and that included fillers. The Sunday paper sold for seven cents.

He pulled into the left lane of traffic from the rest stop. "I am still not certain as to where the bodega was located that Munoz worked," Joyce said.

"I thought you said you were there at the bodega," Elizabeth said.

"I only got bits and pieces from the newspapers and what the DA's detective described to me. He talked about the refrigerator in the basement that held the cold cuts. That's bullshit. There were no refrigerators in the basements of the bodegas. If they sold cold cuts at all. They would have the cold cuts displayed and their inventory was what was displayed. They sold newspapers, cigarettes, cigars, beer, soda, milk, bottled water had not been invented yet, some coffee, usually the instant kind such as Folgers and Sanka. They sold Twinkies, Ring Dings, Yankee Doodles, Devil Dogs, Yodels, Coconut Snowballs, Coffee Cakes, which were stocked by the van driver from Hostess Cupcake company. The potato chips, cheese doodles, but they were in single serving bags, there were no Doritos and the like, only barbecue potato chips for those who dared were stocked by the delivery man from the company which was Wise. There was a section for candies, but that was always directly in front of the register for the owner to watch over the children after school. They did have some boxed cereals on the shelves along with individual toilet paper and paper towel rolls. They were the basic necessities for the neighborhood residents.

"The owner himself would do his shopping at warehouse stores throughout Manhattan. They purchased the beer and soda that was needed at the distributer on Houston Street and Avenue C or on East Fifth Street off of Avenue C. They only held a week's supply in their store. There was no need to stock up. All the items were stored in a back room. If Fausto worked at the store, it would have been when the owner went shopping and he helped him carry the items into his van and then into the store, and that was always around six to ten o'clock in the morning.

"I cannot say this often enough, there was no reason for Fausto to go into the basement of the store, much less with a little boy. There was nothing down there and then for Fausto to say he threw Nate's backpack on top of the refrigerator is total bullshit.

People didn't get their coffee until they got out of the subway and were near their office or work site. Today we see people walking around the streets with their ubiquitous cup of coffee in hand. It wasn't that way years ago. The coffee trucks were always parked outside of the large office buildings, much to the displeasure of the building's food service manager. The workers got their cup of coffee and buttered roll for seventy-five cents and walked into their office building. There were no large office buildings in SoHo, just small residential lofts or the five-story tenements. Forget the tourists, there was nothing in the area for them to see. Some of the office workers in the commercial buildings on Varick Street ventured over to SoHo for lunch, but that was it. The residential population down in the financial district was nonexistent, they still lived in New Jersey, Upper Manhattan, or Long Island."

"I think I just did a crash course in Manhattan history," Joyce said.

"If it is true and Fausto worked in the bodega on the corner of Prince and West Broadway, they would have to sell potato chips by the chip because there was no room for a full bag to pass by someone else inside. It is now a clothing store."

"I guess the owner of that bodega fell into the category of the 'take the garbage home' store owner," she said.

"Exactly, there would only be the rare occasion for a thirty-five-gallon trash bag," Joyce said.

"Did anyone ask Fausto to show the jury just exactly how big a thirty-five gallon was?" Elizabeth asked.

"I don't think he ever took the witness stand," Joyce said.

"Did anyone ever put a detective on the stand and ask him or her to show the jury how large a thirty-five-gallon trash bag was?" she asked.

"I see where you are going with this," Joyce said.

Elizabeth took a sip of her coffee and looked out the window as her husband drove to the Outerbridge Crossing.

18

The Next Morning
Joyce's House

Joyce struggled with the bedsheets, it's another episode where he was visited by the parents of the little boy from SoHo. He slammed his fist against his pillow. He wanted them to end—the dreams. His failing to find the little boy, it all had subsided and somehow went away until Fausto Munoz came forward and told friends he had killed the little boy from SoHo. Munoz worked at the store near Nate Zapata's school bus stop and everyone believed his story. The story was that he talked with the little boy and took him into the basement of the store to get him a bottle of soda. He said he killed little Nate in the basement, then he recanted his statement.

Joyce's mind screamed at the stupidity of how the district attorney was hinging her case on the sole testimony of Munoz. Joyce read bits and pieces of newspaper articles of the first trial and he kept shaking his head and thinking, "Hey, I was there, why haven't they talked with me and the others cops from NSU II." *We were there that night,* he thought as he wrapped himself around his pillow. Joyce threw his sheets to the side and stepped out of his bed. He put on his running shirt and shorts, stretched for ten minutes, and went running. He wasn't certain how long his run would take. He knew it would be over when he had thought everything through.

Joyce finished his fourteen-mile run in two hours. He wanted a tall cup of coffee and to hold his wife. He got the coffee but his wife had gone shopping. He ran into the shower, did a "dance around," then checked the internet some addresses of the locations he needed to visit. It was back to the cemeteries again, possibly the last time. He was down to a few that only could have been visited by the Zapatas to bury their son and return in time to call the police. It suddenly struck Joyce like a rock hitting him on his head. *What if they didn't bury their son at a cemetery but simply dug up some dirt in a forest and buried him?* he thought.

Joyce chose to visit five small cemeteries in and around the Catskill Mountains. Beth Israel cemetery would be his last. If he did not find Nate Zapata's remains in any of these five, there would be no hope for Munoz. Joyce would need to know when to use his private investigator business cards or leave them in his car and use his retired NYPD lieutenant shield and identification. He slowed when he spotted the cast-iron four-foot fencing alongside the road. It was the early days of fall, and he may have to return another day. He had forgotten to factor in pushing his clocks back an hour. He had put all the locations on his computer late one night, after Elizabeth had gone to bed. It was the time he did his best tactical work.

Beth Israel Cemetery

He looked at the plaque on the column of the archway which defined the entrance to the cemetery. It was light green in color, which indicated that it was made of copper. The words Beth Israel Cemetery were in raised lettering but barely noticeable from a few feet away. The wrought-iron gates hadn't seen paint in over twenty years. A small stone house stood to the right of the entrance. It had a wooden entrance door that also needed a fresh coat of paint. It was the cemetery's office. Joyce looked around the entire seven-acre cemetery. There were no toolsheds, tractors, backhoes, to be seen. He slid his holstered gun off his belt and slid it under his seat as he parked his red Mustang Convertible at the curb, just in front of the side window. He hoped a middle-aged widow would be working in the office, as they usually did. He opened the door and a tiny bell jingled. It was almost the way Elizabeth described her great-grandparents' old grocery to him. Their store was in Windsor Terrace, Brooklyn.

Joyce learned the art of smiling from Elizabeth. "Hi, I'm Bob Joyce. I am a retired NYPD lieutenant. I have recently taken an ancestry DNA test. I did it because I thought I was one hundred percent Irish. I am forty-three percent Jewish. Ancestry gave me a couple of locations where my relatives may have lived and possibly died," he blurted out.

"That was a lot, but you are not wearing a ring, not married," the middle-aged woman, who sported a wig, said. She was sitting, but Joyce guessed her height as five feet five inches tall.

"A widower," Joyce said. "And you?"

"A widow."

"Sorry, but I know I have to get on with my life," Joyce said.

The woman sat up in her chair and slid it over to the reception area. "So how long is she . . . ?"

"Three years."

"That's long enough, you should start seeking a mate," she said.

Joyce looked down at his notes. "Why, are you available?"

"That is why I work here. So what can I do for you, handsome, besides cooking you a great dinner with some wine?"

"My great-great-grandfather lived in this area, back in the late 1880s."

"That was about the time when this cemetery was established. Cholera and yellow fever killed so many Jewish people up here," she said.

"The Irish half of me lost all my grandfather's siblings to tuberculosis."

"You are Irish, I love the Irish. I mean, their accent. You must be Catholic too," she said.

"Yes, why?" Joyce said carefully.

"All we have here are Jewish men, I have always wanted to meet a Catholic man and now I have met an Irish Catholic one."

"I dated a Jewish girl when I was a teenager. Her name was Rachael Gordon. She came from Israel and stayed with her grandparents, who were holocaust survivors. They lived in a house next door to ours. She stayed for a month one summer. We were friends from the first day we met. When she had to go back to Israel, I was so upset."

"How did you meet your wife?"

"A friend introduced us. We had a rocky start but eventually we became friends and got married. One Friday evening, my wife was on her way home from work when a man jumped out of a car and tried to grab her purse. My wife fought and was dragged alongside his car, until she gave up her bag, but it was too late, she slid under the rear wheels of the car and was run over and killed."

The woman took a deep breath and looked directly at Joyce. "I am so sorry."

"What about you?" Joyce said.

"We got married, then he decided to go back to Israel and fight in the Israeli army. He died the first day," she said.

"From a gunshot?" Joyce asked innocently.

"I wish, he had a heart attack after he heard that a shot had been fired. He is buried at the back of the cemetery. It was the cheapest grave that I could afford," she said.

"No one else?" he asked.

"Have you seen the crop of men here? Leftover, pickled cattle. Nothing I would want to share my bed with. Oh, I live alone, in my own house, that my parents left to me, which wasn't much."

"I detect an invitation," Joyce said.

"I'm not available on Friday afternoon and all day Saturday, my faith . . . ," she said meekly.

"I know that from my old neighborhood growing up. Benji was my best friend's name, and we were friends all summer except the year Rachael came to visit. Benji's father was the rabbi from a synagogue five houses from mine."

"I love your blue eyes," she said.

"Okay, putting our marriage plans aside, is there a chance you could find my great-grandparents for me?"

"It's only me here today. I'll let you look through the files but you have to promise me it will only be your family's files," she said.

Joyce jokingly hunched his shoulders and gave her a creepy look as he rubbed his hands together.

"Why are they secret files? By the way, what is your name?"

"Sharon Rosenberg," she said proudly.

"Sharon, that's a pretty name. Now where are the old files?" Joyce asked.

She walked over to her desk, unlocked it, and opened the bottom drawer. She removed a key which hung on a small hook at the back of her drawer, hidden by mounds of loose files, long awaiting to be put back in their file folders. She pulled on the overhead chain which turned on the simple forty-watt bulb. She took the key and opened the closet in the back of the office. That key also unlocked the filing cabinet, which had been turned around so the drawers opened to the wall. She turned the cabinet around and unlocked the bottom drawer. She removed the long file box and placed it on her desk. She looked down at the files then over to Joyce.

"These are all the people we know of who are buried here. The cemetery book is no longer here. I don't know what happened to it and I didn't care, until the family lawyer read the will up to the part where I was given control of the cemetery. I had no idea what my responsibilities were. I called around to other cemeteries and some gave me hints but the biggest problem I had was there was no book."

"Do people come here often, to visit?"

"Not really, we are closed most of the time. Today we had a funeral, so we stayed open the entire day. If someone calls and says that they would like to visit a relative's grave, I will drive over and open the gates and stay in the office the entire day to do paperwork."

"I don't see any gardeners or other workers, you know, the guys who mow the grass and dig the graves."

"My uncle Joshua Levy owned this cemetery, and did all the work himself, except for mowing and digging the graves. He hired someone to do that work. He kept this cemetery open from Sunday to Friday. He died three years ago and left me with its care," she said.

Joyce smiled for a moment. "Do you mow the grass?" Joyce asked jokingly.

"Noooo, silly. My uncle paid Mr. Antunnicci fifty dollars to dig the graves and fill them in later. His son mows the grass for free. They keep the grass cuttings and use it to feed their cows. He owns that big farm, the one you drove by, to get here."

Joyce thought for a moment. *I gotta chat with that man.*

"Does he have a first name, this, er, Mr. Antunnicci?"

"Rocco, sometimes he likes people to call him Mr. Rocco because they can't pronounce his last name."

"Oh, I understand that. I'll just look through these cards for his name, my grandfather's."

"What was your great-grandfather's last name?" Sharon asked.

Joyce's heart skipped a beat, he had to think fast. "He was from Poland and there are seven different variations of the spelling of the family name. To this day,

I can't pronounce it properly, or any of the versions," Joyce said, causing Sharon to giggle.

"I know the feeling, it happens every time someone looks for a long-lost relative, back at the turn of the century. What letter does the last name begin with?" she asked.

"An A, C, or an S, maybe a KJ, it could even start with a Z. I just don't know. I know it is against protocol to look at the cards and the book is missing, but I promise, I'll just look at the names only," Joyce said boyishly. He knew he hit the soft spot, she went for the files.

"I'm not supposed to let anyone look at all the files. It is a privacy issue and a New York State Law."

She walked the files to the back of the small office and put them onto a desk where no one but she could see. Joyce sat down in the chair and put his file folder next to his chair. He knew he may have hit a jackpot. This was his last shot. He had visited every cemetery in a seventy-two-hundred-square-mile area. It would be getting dark in two hours. He needed time to read. He wondered what she would ask him to do if he needed her to open the cemetery to see the cards again.

Joyce began reading the grave cards. Fifteen minutes later, he knew that it would not be as easy as he thought, the cards were not in either alphabetical or chronological order. It would be a test of wills, his and Sharon's.

He needed to take a chance and started pushing through the older card files. He turned to look at Sharon, who was busy painting her toe nails. Joyce smiled because Elizabeth would always ask him to do her toe nails when she wanted to make love. Joyce would always make the excuse that he didn't want to get any polish on her long robe so he would open the two sides of her robe completely. He would slowly start his routine. Toenails until they dried, then an inner-thigh massage, then.....

He returned his attention to the cards as his vision of Elizabeth, lying naked disappeared. He tried to do a quick flip of the cards but it was no help, he would need more time. He would have to read each card carefully, but Sharon was now painting her toes on her other foot. He would not be finished in time. He glanced back at Sharon who was waiting for the polish to dry. Her dress was now at the top of both legs. He finished reading the last card. "*That's it. Nothing on these cards to indicate when, where, or even if Mr. Rocco ever did open a grave on May 24 or 25, 1979. It's over. This was my last cemetery, there is no other cemetery I can check. I have no more options,* he thought. He didn't want to give up and walk away. He needed another look, this time a slow look but how could he do it with Sharon right near him. She finished putting on her shoes and straightened her dress. "What, no lacquer finish. I used to put it on for my wife when she went out for the evening with her friends," Joyce said.

"I never thought of that. If you would be a dear and finish them for me, I'll go back to my house and get the lacquer."

Suddenly the file draw fell from the desk, spilling the grave cards onto the floor. "I'm sorry, I don't know how that happened," he said. "I was watching you watching me and you never moved. Did you finish looking for your relative's grave locations?"

"I was halfway through looking at the cards. I'll stay here and look through the cards again, if you don't mind." "I guess it will be okay. I'll be back in twenty minutes or so."

Joyce turned to look at the pile of cards lying on the floor. He was mindful to look behind and under the desk for any of the cards.

He had all the cards aligned properly but not in alphabetical, chronological or geographical order. That process would take up valuable time. He placed the file drawer on his lap and removed the cards one at a time. He read each card and placed it face down. This continued for twenty minutes. Joyce wondered if his search would end without ever finding the remains of little Nate Zapata. He gently pulled another card out and read the face. The small index didn't feel right. It was different, more solid than the others. He held the card in his hand and gently pressed his thumb against it. He went back to the last card from the file and placed it into his free hand, it bent easily and was slightly lighter than the other card. He took another card from the pile, it too bent easily. He put that card back on the pile and put his attention to the card in question. He looked at the side of the card. He was holding two cards perfectly aligned. He took a single edge razor from his shield case and gently pushed it between the two cards. He looked at the first card, it had three dates for grave openings/closings but none coincided with what Joyce needed. The second card had the sticky substance on its edges. The grave number, if in sequence would indicate that it was for the adjoining grave. More importantly, the card indicated that the grave S. F, R.M, G.21 (section F, row M, grave 21) had been opened on May 24/25, 1979. It had been an overnight dig for Mr. Rocco. He took out his mini-camera and took four photos of both the front and back of the two cards. Joyce would need a map of all the graves in the cemetery.

Joyce heard Sharon's car pull into her dedicated parking spot. He continued looking for any other "double" grave cards. The tiny bell tinkled. "I'm back," she said proudly. "I put the lacquer coat during my conversation with a grave owner, no need for your help, this time," she said.

"Sharon, did your uncle keep a hard-covered bound book with the chronological order of the burials?"

When I took over, I looked for it but I never found it. The cards are all I have."

"How about his house?"

"My uncle's house caught fire a month after he died. The fire killed his wife, my aunt, and destroyed everything in it."

"Maybe he gave the book to Mr. Rocco. I'll pass by his house on my way home and ask him," Joyce said.

"Mr. Rocco should not be in possession of the book, it is against the law," Sharon said adamantly.

"Relax, if I find it, it would help you, because those cards are in terrible order," Joyce said.

"That was my fault. I brought in my sister-in-law to work for me, she was a drunk, and one day, she took all the files out of the drawer to show me what she could do and she dropped all of them on the floor. She just grabbed bunches of them and pushed them into the drawer. They were upside down, backward, bent, torn, ripped, or crushed. I haven't had time to put them in order. I hope you found what you were looking for," she said.

"Do you have a map of the entire cemetery, with all the grave locations?" Joyce asked.

"Are you looking for a particular grave?"

"I have a couple of possibilities, but right now, I just needed a map of the entire cemetery with all the grave locations. The map would have been in the book in some cemeteries, others print out the maps for the visitors so they can locate the graves of their relatives on their own."

"I'll pull up the map on my computer and print it out for you. When can we go to dinner?"

Joyce took the printed copy of the cemetery map and looked into her eyes.

"I have a trial coming up, once it's over, I'll come up for you and take you to dinner in Manhattan."

"If there is anything else that you need, please feel free to call me on my cell."

"I may take you up on that offer. Thanks," Joyce said.

On a Dirt Road, Leading to a Farmhouse

Joyce parked his Mustang in front of the white clapboard house as the screen door opened. A thin man about twenty-eight years old wearing jeans and a NY Mets jersey-type shirt stepped out onto the wooden porch. "Can I help you, sir?" he asked. "By the way, nice car."

Joyce smiled at the young man and approached him with his hand extended. "Hi, I'm Bob Joyce. I'm a retired lieutenant from the NYPD, you must be Carmine."

"So why are you here?" Carmine said coldly.

"How is your dad? Look, I'm going to be honest with you. I'm just fishing for information right now. Did your father keep a record for each time he dug graves for the cemetery?"

"Thanks for asking about Dad, but he is in the final stages of liver/pancreatic cancer. He will be spending the rest of his time in *his* cemetery soon."

"I understand, but I am working on a case that has nothing to do with your dad. I think."

"You think?" Carmine said quizzically.

Joyce knew that he needed to approach the next question carefully.

"Back in the late seventies, a boy went missing on his way to school. I've checked the cemetery records for over a hundred cemeteries, here in New York and New Jersey. There is only one grave that had been dug for a burial that morning, and that one is over in Beth Israel Cemetery. The name on the grave card does not match the family name of the boy who went missing. I believe his father was a cousin of the cemetery owner, who died a few years ago. His daughter Sharon and I are good friends. I am not looking to get anyone in trouble, besides the statute of limitations has long since expired. I would like the boy to have a proper burial."

"Why do you want to know if my father had anything to do with the improper burial of someone?"

"Look, I'm not certain there is another body under the coffin. If there is nothing under the coffin, you can close it up. I will be on my way, because I will have run out of places where the little boy could have been buried."

"I just don't understand why you need to know," Carmine said. Joyce was doing his best to stay calm. He didn't want to go through the process of calling the state police before he saw the records Mr. Antunnicci kept, if he kept any at all.

"Okay, here it is, there is a guy, a Hispanic guy has admitted to killing a little boy. It's been in the newspapers," Joyce said.

"But the guy now says he didn't do it," Carmine interrupted. "You said the statute of limitations was over, so why is he on trial?" Carmine asked.

Joyce took a deep breath and closed his eyes and he thought, *I know he did admit to killing the little boy, but that was after three detectives sat him at a table in a very small room and hammered him with questions. Each detective took their turn. His back was against two walls in a corner.* He suddenly remembered the call he received many years earlier. It was at the start of the Mollen Commission hearings. Jack Newfield, a columnist for the *New York Post*, had written an article about Joyce who told him about a book he had just completed and in the book he got to kill a bad cop. The title of the article was "Good Cop Nabs the Bad Cop by the Tale." Detectives at the Mollen Commission picked up on the story and a lieutenant contacted him for a meeting with the lead prosecutor involved in the hearings. Joyce agreed and secretly met with Leslie Cornfeld and a lieutenant in a large conference room in a building located at the tip of Manhattan. The view from the conference room window was beautiful.

Joyce first met with the lieutenant and then with Leslie Cornfeld. She was five feet five inches and the human version of a pit bull. Cornfeld asked a few polite and soft questions, then she went for Joyce's throat. She kept badgering him about his arrests and how he lied about some of the details of the arrest because every cop lied in some form or another. Joyce stayed his ground, when it came to his integrity, though he always remembered the feeling he had after as the badgering continued. He, at one point, stopped listening to Cornfeld's questions and somehow doubted himself and wondered if he ever did lie about an arrest. He snapped out of the fog and looked directly at her. His strongly worded statement was enough for the other lieutenant. He gently placed his hand on Cornfeld's left arm. It was a signal to stop the line of questioning. Cornfeld went back to her puppy role and started to schedule in Joyce for his testimony. Joyce had other plans. "I'll think about it and give you a call with my decision." Cornfeld almost had a stroke. Joyce got up from his chair and walked out of the office and building. He still had Cornfeld's business card in his hand. Then he opened his eyes and let out the air. He understood how Fausto Munoz, someone with limited intelligence, could fall for the detective's trap.

"Because he said he killed the boy by strangling him. That's murder and there is no statute of limitations on murder. He's a little simple and admitted to killing the boy after a couple of detectives kept at him, until he admitted doing it. The boy's body has never been recovered. I believe something happened to the boy. His father may have taken him here and buried his son in an opened grave. Sharon said that no one else was buried in the grave beside the person listed on her records," Joyce said again softly.

Carmine took his hands out of his pants pockets and held them to his mouth. He blew on them and then wiped his hands on his denim jeans and extended one hand to Joyce.

"Two hundred to open and two hundred to close it," Carmine said to Joyce. They shook hands, Carmine went to release his hand, but Joyce held on to it momentarily. Joyce sensed the nervousness in the boy as his hand began to shake.

"I need to see the book," Joyce said and released his grip.

"My father kept his records in his bedroom closet. He is in a coma, so I doubt he will object. I have always wondered what was in the book ever since I was a kid. He warned us never to go into his closet, because there was a man in there who would take us and bury us in an empty grave, and then have a coffin placed on top of us in case we tried to escape. That kept all of us out."

Carmine left and returned three minutes later with a broad smile on his face. "My father was awake, so I asked him if I could let you take a look at the book. He smiled and nodded his head yes."

Joyce opened the book slowly. It was a simple marble-bound notebook. Some of the pages were soiled, others looked as though they had been wet. Joyce carefully flipped through the pages before finding the entry for Nate. He looked up and smiled at Carmine.

"It looks like he stopped digging graves eighteen months ago," Joyce said.

"That was when his doctor told him he had cancer. He told me that he was handing over the responsibilities of digging graves on that day."

Joyce looked at Carmine. "All the handwriting is the same," Joyce said.

"I intended to start my own book, instead I simply continued with the same style of entries and copying my father's handwriting, I now continue my father's work without interruption. In the beginning, my father looked at each entry, making sure I completed them by his rules. Now he can't read, so I show him my entries and he simply nods his head slightly. My father made me swear that I would never leave a grave until I had finished making my entries in my book. I have respected my father's wishes and have always remained until the entries have been completed."

"That would explain the dirt and the old wet pages," Joyce said.

Carmine smiled. "It could be pouring rain as my father stood there and got soaked making the entries. Then he would go into the kitchen and take off his clothes off and walk up the bedroom to change. The only clothes my father wore were four pairs of overalls, four white T-shirts for the summer, and three flannel shirts for the winter."

"I guess he wasn't a churchgoing man, or did he wear his overalls to church?" Joyce asked.

"No, Dad had one black suit which was always pressed, along with two white shirts, one short sleeve for summer, and the long sleeve for winter. There aren't that many Catholics still living here. We had to travel to church in a pickup truck, we sat in the back, all four of us. I am the only one who has stayed with dad. When he goes, I will take over the farm, I kind of like it here."

Joyce opened the pages to the date of Nate's disappearance. There it was, Mr. Rocco's entry. Section F, Row M, Grave 21.

"He dug a grave eight feet deep and put a small boy into the grave and buried the body under two feet of dirt where the coffin would be placed. Then he would fill the entire opening with dirt. He would spread the excess dirt over the surrounding graves." Joyce noticed the slight quivering of Mr. Rocco's hand on the last two sentences of the entry. *He must have felt some guilt at that point.* He compared the picture of the grave card on his mini camera to the entry Mr. Rocco made. They were a match.

Joyce wanted to return the book to Carmine, but changed his mind. Joyce closed the book and held it tightly in his hand.

"Carmine, since your father will no longer be using this book, could I hold on to it for a while? I promise I will give it back to you in its entirety," Joyce asked.

"Lieutenant, I made a promise to my father that I would not leave the grave until I made the entry. I cannot break my promise," Carmine said.

Joyce opened the book, took a photo of the entry, closed the book, and handed it back. Joyce began to walk toward his car but stopped and turned to Carmine.

"Remember we shook hands and made a deal that you would open the grave for me," Joyce said. Carmine had a blank stare on his face. Joyce had remembered his days with Benji and Joyce learned much about the Jewish religion, including the fact that a handshake between two Jewish men was sacred and honored as a written contract.

19

Manhattan District Attorney's Office Surprise

Hal Whithers was the new prosecutor in the case against Fausto Munoz for the murder of Nate Zapata. A journalist for an underground prisoner freedom movement had interviewed Joyce nine months earlier about Joyce's involvement.

Joyce read the daily reports of the first trial. There seemed to be some confusion about who did what and whether the patrol officers may have overlooked something, or was it the detectives who failed to notice an apparent mistake. Joyce e-mailed a letter to the editor of one of the New York newspapers, in fact, he cc'd all the New York City newspapers with his opinion of the apparent dustup between the cops and the detectives. Joyce's letter to the editor was printed in the Daily News.

One local paper had an intern read the letters to the editor from all the city newspapers and pick out the ones from Staten Island. Another intern was assigned to interview the writer. She selected Joyce's complaint, and she wrote a three-quarter-page story about Joyce and how he searched for the little boy from SoHo that first night in the local newspaper.

Karen Carlucci, the initial prosecutor, would be Whithers's special assistant during this new trial. They both sat behind the large conference room table as Joyce entered.

"Hi, Bob, it's been a while," Carlucci said.

"Karen, do you know the witness?" Whithers snapped.

"We worked together on an issue after I first left the office. It was on a professional basis, nothing personal, I promise," Carlucci said.

"We only talked politics and not the case. It was my first time publicly supporting a politician running for office. Everyone who knows me knows I have no love for politicians. Are you folks going to use me at the trial?" Joyce asked bluntly.

"Sorry, Bob, but your testimony will be more of a liability than an asset on this case. So it is a no-go, and please refrain from coming to the courtroom. Thank you for your time," Carlucci said.

"Fine, no hard feelings. I just wanted to set aside some time," Joyce said and grabbed his clutch bag.

"Bobby Joyce, are you giving up so easily on this case?" Carlucci asked.

"Oh no, no way. I will be in touch," Joyce said

"Sorry, Lieutenant," Whithers said.

Joyce walked out of the office and dialed the office of William Careswell. He waited for the usual two rings before the receptionist hit the button for Joyce's call. She began her opening line for the office introduction. "Stop, it's me, Lieutenant Joyce, put me through to Billy's office now," Joyce snapped. The receptionist recognized his voice and put the call through to the office of Billy Careswell.

"Hey, Lieutenant, good to hear from you. I understand you are still interested in the Munoz case," Billy Careswell said.

"I wasn't sure if you were going to use me. I just wanted to set my calendar straight," Joyce said.

"Sorry, Lieutenant, we don't need you at this moment. Thanks for your input about that night. You've been very helpful," Careswell said carefully. Joyce was now free to do what he wanted to do almost forty years earlier.

Whithers turned to look at Carlucci. "He told me the first day I met him that he was there the first night. I told him what I thought, that I believed Fausto Munoz was guilty of murdering Nate Zapata. Besides, he never really showed an interest in testifying," she said.

"What type of cop was he, and could he have stood a background scrutiny, if we did call him?" Whithers said.

"He was a very active cop, sergeant, and lieutenant," she said.

"No, I mean when he testified before a jury," he said.

"I never had a case with him, he retired before I had a chance to work with him. I did check some of his case files and talked with a few of the prosecutors from our office who knew him when he was a cop. Some of them are bureau chiefs and remember him well. He was always on point. In one case, his testimony before a grand jury on a drug case was used as an instructional tool for all new incoming special narcotics prosecutors."

"Why didn't you want him to testify?"

"He told me what he believes happened, and I couldn't allow the jury to hear his story," she said.

"Why didn't you call him to testify in the first trial?"

"I didn't know he existed until we worked together," Carlucci said.

"Should I be worried about him?" he asked.

Seven Weeks Earlier
Basement Library of Law Firm Alcort, Ventura, Johnson, Evans & O'Neill

Careswell walked into the basement of his office building, hoping to see Larry. He had self-doubt about defending the case. Fausto Munoz would be on trial for the second time for the murder of Nate Zapata. Careswell knew Munoz's defense was weak the first time the case went to trial. Now it was anemic. Careswell heard a noise from the back of the basement library. He called out, "Larry, is that you?"

"Yeah, Mr. C, I'm putting my things together."

"Why?"

"I'm moving on," Larry said.

"Bu . . . but why."

"You don't need me anymore," Larry said.

"The hell I don't. I'm going to trial and it is going to be a difficult one. I've put a lot more work into the case but I'm going to need your help."

"Mr. C, we have known each other for only a short time. I trust your judgment. Maybe now you need to trust mine. Today is my last day here. I will not be here after six this evening. Trust your judgment, use free will."

"But you . . . you have a gift," Careswell said.

"Someone else needs my help for a while, and they will be needing it shortly. They could die if I don't help. I will be working every night on this one," Larry said.

Careswell closed his Redweld and extended his hand, Larry took it. "May God speed," Careswell said.

Larry didn't say a word but smiled and patted Careswell on his shoulder as the elevator doors opened.

Joyce's House
Later That Evening

Joyce sat on his couch, his Jack Russell Terrier named "Jack" was fighting with an imaginary adversary, a stuffed animal toy. Elizabeth sat casually across on the couch from her husband as he gently messaged her legs. Their son and daughter had married and given them three grandchildren, a boy and two girls—so far.

Elizabeth took a small sip of wine from her glass and put it back on the end table.

"Bob, let me get this straight. You called both the district attorney, who is prosecuting the case, and the defense attorney for Fausto, whatever his name is, and neither is going to call you to testify."

"I don't know why, that's what they do."

"And you can't think of a reason as to why they don't want to call you."

"All right, look, the way I remember that night, our van was parked on the west side of West Broadway, about thirty feet north of Spring Street. Our van was a block south of where the prosecution says we were supposedly parked that Friday night. Our van was the only one there that night, despite what people have written. Some say there were three hundred cops that night searching for Nate along with bloodhounds. Nope, that's a lie. The twelve of us NSU II cops were the only uniforms there. We were the Temporary Headquarters Vehicle that night. Detective Brass and others came to our vehicle and remained there as did the little boy's father, Alan, who gave out pictures of his son to us. Some of the guys were paired with the detectives to do building apartment door knocks to see if anyone saw Nate. We were the THV that first night. I went shopping in SoHo to use the gift card I found. I went to the spot where the NYPD detectives say the THV was, but that's not true. We were the THV, and we were a block south of the spot, where they say the school bus stop for Nate Zapata was located. Their THV location would be adjacent to where the store was located, where Fausto Munoz says he took the little boy into the basement. That's bullshit. I went to the location where the detectives say Fausto worked. We had our roll call at the end of our tour inside the store, which is now a clothing store. It would have been too cramped for us. The other location, a block south, has also been transformed into a clothing store, but it had the room for us, the same room the grocery store had that we got thrown out of. I also remember the outside of the location, at the curb. The decline in the sidewalk was noticeable. One of the female cops made a comment that I still remember today. I remember I had a strange feeling when I stood at the curb and all the other cops were standing much taller than me. That has rarely happened to me."

Elizabeth smiled and took another sip of wine and removed the glass from her lip. "Now you know how I feel when I walk next to you."

Joyce reached over and took a deep breath and then exhaled to take a long draw of wine.

"How many times have I told you about me leaving my raincoat in some of the bodegas on my foot post? The owners would have to call the precinct to remind me to come and pick it up."

"Many times."

"That's right. I made friends with the store owners when I was in NSU, that's what I was supposed to do. Not only I, but all of us, it just seemed the 'I' was all the store owners ever talked with. I would go into the store to get warm and then go back out to patrol the street. While I was in the store, I noticed there were always two workers in the store by the cash register. I know that, because if there was only one person working, and I walked in, the first thing they would ask is for me to stand by the register while they went to the bathroom. There was always an owner and a close relative working or, in a rare case, a worker on the floor and two relatives behind the counter. The store the detectives say was the store where Fausto worked, was way too tiny. Two workers could have easily worked the floor and the register. The store where I believe, no, I know, we were in was much bigger, but not so much bigger to need a third person.

"Fausto claimed he was a worker in a bodega and the owners gave him the keys to the basement, where they stored their supplies and it was where he took the little boy. That's bullshit. The owner would never give the keys to the basement to a worker. There is no way that Fausto Munoz took little Nate Zapata into the basement without the store owner knowing. The glass window by the register overlooked the diamond steel gates which led to the basement and those doors never remained open. No freaken' way, never.

"That's why I gotta go do my own thing on this," Joyce said coldly.

"We have been married a long time, Bob. I know you, and you are on a mission to blow this case wide open and you don't even have a smile on your face."

"Liz, that has to stay in this house. The kids can't know until I say so."

"Bob, I can't tell you how many times I have said this, but I want you to go for it. The way you do it, your way."

20

Warnings
State Supreme Court
111 Centre Street
Part 60

Six Weeks Earlier

A court officer slammed his hand against the large file cabinet, which was located next to the door to the judge's chambers. The courtroom was packed with newspaper and television reporters, along with the curious. Alan and Arlene sat on a wooden bench located immediately behind the prosecutor's table. A thick wooden railing divided the viewer's space from the "well" area, where the actual court proceedings were held.

"All rise! Come to order! Hear ye, hear ye, all persons having business in this Criminal Court Part 7, held in and for the County of New York, draw forth, give your attendance, and ye shall be heard. The Honorable Judge George Ruttenberger presiding," the Supreme Court officer announced in a loud voice.

The judge welcomed and thanked the members of the jury for their service. He also thanked the defense and the prosecution, then he turned to those in attendance.

"Today is the beginning of the end for the family of the deceased. I will not allow any outbursts from *any-one* in my court. If you do, I will have you removed and arrested."

He looked out over the entire courtroom; as he did, he said, "Does everyone understand?" Everyone nodded confirmation that they understood. The court interpreter repeated the declaration in Spanish and in French. The judge motioned for both the prosecution and the defense to approach his desk, a formality. They stood and walked over to the judge's bench.

"Is there going to be any surprises during this trial, like some unknown witness?" Billy Careswell looked over to Carlucci, they both nodded their heads in unison.

"Judge, could we have a meeting on that, in your chambers?" Carlucci asked.

Judge Ruttenberger stood up from his high-back chair and looked over those in attendance. "We will have a brief ten-minute meeting in my chambers. Sorry for the interruption."

The judge walked into his chambers and went behind his desk and sat in his leather chair. He kept his robe on.

"Okay, when were you going to tell me this new information?" Ruttenberger asked.

"Well, Judge, this happened sort of by accident. A friend of mine was running for a political spot in the primary, and I was supporting her, along with a bunch of other people. One of those people happened to be a retired NYPD lieutenant. He introduced himself and immediately let me know he was one of the first responding officers to search for Nate Zapata," she said.

Ruttenberger let his disappointment show, as he let out a long breath of air.

"Was this officer someone who just responded to the emergency of a missing boy and then left?"

"No, Judge, he told me he had conducted searches of Nate's building and others buildings in the neighborhood. He also informed me he had talked in length with the defense and I thought this was important for the lieutenant to talk to the prosecution also. That was before I was called back to help with this case."

"I thought you said he was an officer, like a cop?" Ruttenberger said coldly. No one said a word. "I treat lieutenants differently when they come to trial."

"He met with my co-counsel a while ago. He told me he had been at Nate's residence that first night. The lieutenant was very cooperative but we both agree his statements would confuse the jury. Counsel and I agreed not to enter him on the list of potential witnesses," Carlucci said.

"Counselors, and I mean both sides, I want to talk with this retired lieutenant ASAP. We will proceed with the case, but before I accept a verdict from this jury, I will need to speak to him," Ruttenberger said.

"Judge, I blew him off and he has not returned my calls. I believe he may be using a cheap phone as my detective said. The prosecutor's investigators have experienced the same problem with trying to contact the lieutenant," Careswell said.

Ruttenberger looked down at his desk for a moment. He started nodding his head. "I want both sides to aggressively try to contact this lieutenant. Do you both understand and agree?" he said. Both sides said yes.

"No word of this to the press, and that is an order. If something is said, I will hold you both in contempt and then you can figure out who gave out the information. Now let's get back to the courtroom. I will lead the two of you out." The court officer repeated his announcement.

New York State Police Barracks
Troop M
Present Day

Joyce sat with a book on his lap as he waited for Trooper Detective Collins. Collins and Joyce's nephew had met during their marine basic training and continued on to the New York State Trooper Academy. It was Joyce's nephew Christopher who returned to active duty only to be cut down by a sniper trying to save Collins's life in the process.

"Lieutenant Joyce, how are you doing today?" Collins said as he entered the barracks office. He stood proudly at attention as he waited for Joyce's hand. His uniform was impeccable.

"Easy on the lieutenant crap, I'm retired," Joyce leaned over and whispered.

"Not here you're not. Everyone keeps their rank until their 'final' roll call."

"I like that," Joyce said.

"Let's go into my office."

Joyce followed the detective down the long hallway into a small back office. Papers were piled on every chair and across the entire space on his desk. Joyce looked around the office and smiled. “The jobs may be different but the paperwork is the same. Every NYPD detective’s desk looks as yours does,” Joyce said.

“I thought I was the only one. My lieutenant is always breaking my balls to clean up my office, but as soon as I clear a case and file it away, two more are handed to me.”

Collins looked around his office. “Just put the files from that chair and put them on the floor and pull the chair up to my desk,” Collins said as he removed two piles of file folders from the top of his desk and placed them on the cabinet behind his desk. He pointed back to the two piles. “I will forget where I put those by tomorrow and it will take me hours to find them.”

Joyce pulled the chair to the desk and began. “My request is going to be simple. I need you to hook me up with a cop-friendly judge. I am going to need permission to open a grave at Beth Israel Cemetery.”

“Beth Israel is a favorite name for cemeteries up here,” Collins said.

“It’s the one just south of Route 28,” Joyce said. Collins made a few notes on his pad and closed the folder.

“Oh, that one. There is something about it, but I am not at liberty to discuss that with you,” Collins said.

“They have that much juice up here?” Joyce asked.

“When she was running for senate, she got a unanimous vote from the entire community.”

“Oh, her, now that she has lost the race for president, her juice will evaporate and the community will have to find someone else to back,” Joyce said.

“Oh, you mean Mr. Sunday,” Collins said.

“We call him the same in the city, useless, but that is a synonym for a politician,” Joyce said.

"Up here, they have a lot of juice with the other politicians," Collins said.

"I drove through the community before I came here. I wanted to get a feel for the people. I don't think they are any better off than my ancestors who came to America in the early 1840s. They live in shanties, no telephones, TV, nada," Joyce said.

"That's the way it is up here. The local rabbi tells them how to vote and they vote without challenging him."

"I guess that was what the Catholic priests did back in the 1800s."

"Time doesn't change much up here," said Collins.

"So tell me, is there a judge I can talk to?" Joyce asked.

"Judge Peter McConville, his family has a long history up here and in the Albany area. He might be able to help."

Joyce sat for a minute before responding. "Could you give him a heads-up call as I drive to his courthouse?" Joyce said.

"He owns the X-Press Gas Station on Route 28. His office is in the rear."

Joyce smiled, leaned over, and shook Collins's hand.

"I love this place," Joyce said. Collins returned a smile.

"You won't meet Barney Fife, but there a plenty of Andy wannabes lurking in the woods," Collins said.

"Next time you are in the city, give me a call, dinner will be on me," Joyce said.

Joyce drove down the two-lane mountainous road for a while until he came upon an X-Press Gas Station. He pulled his Mustang up to the pump and stepped out. A man in dark blue work jeans and blue-and-white striped button-down X-Pressway shirt approached.

OMG, he looks like Andy Griffith, Joyce thought to himself. The gas station attendant stood six feet five inches tall, he had a chiseled face, blue eyes, curly, salt and pepper hair. He extended his hand to Joyce.

"Lieutenant, pleased to meet you, my name is Peter McConville. We can sit in my office and you can tell me what you need," he said.

Joyce hesitated for a moment. "Er, what happens if a customer shows up and wants gas?" Joyce asked innocently.

"They can pay by credit card, which most do. Some pay by cash. They know how to access my cash register and get change if needed," he said.

"You wouldn't last a day in New York City," Joyce said.

"Lieutenant, some of us up here are not so acquainted with the millennium but I am. If you leave my property without paying, it is a while before you can get off the highway. I have cameras in spots you probably didn't see. If gas is dispensed, and either a credit card isn't swiped or the register isn't accessed, I get a notification on my telephone. A picture of the car's front and rear license plate is taken. I notify the local trooper barracks and they grab the thief. It is amazing when the thief has to face both the complainant and the judge at the same time. I usually require the defendant to first pay my tab, the local court fee, and make a donation to the local Catholic church. That last part is between us," McConville said.

I love this place even more, Joyce thought.

"The residents still have power, but not as much," McConville said. "Lieutenant, I got the call, but please, I want you to tell me exactly what you need." McConville sat up in his squeaky wooden chair and put his long, strong arms on his desk. He had an arresting smile which was accentuated by the deep lines in his face. "Lieutenant, what is it that you want?"

"I need a search warrant to dig up a grave," Joyce said nervously.

"Lieutenant, do you really want me to give you permission to dig up a grave, and for God's sakes, why?"

"Judge, there is a man on trial for a second time for murder in the city. He has admitted to killing a little boy who went missing over thirty years ago, and he is now recanting it."

McConville leaned back in his chair and thought for a moment. He stayed in the reclined position as he talked. "I know the case. They are in the process of retrying it as we speak."

"Judge, Fausto Munoz . . . he . . . didn't do it," Joyce said quickly.

"Lieutenant, how do you know that?"

"I believe I know where the little boy's body has been buried since the day he went missing."

"Lieutenant, again, how do you know this?"

"Judge, can we go into your back room and talk?"

McConville's head scowled. "Lieutenant, how do you know I have a back room?"

"Judge, forty-five years ago, a skinny teenager came before you in handcuffs charged with criminal possession of stolen property, a car. You took that teenager into your back room and read him the riot act for being so stupid and hanging out with a career criminal who was also AWOL from the army. The passenger had to spend three days in the local jail before you had the charges dismissed. I was the passenger, that skinny teenager. You had the troopers take the army guy to the local MPs in NYC to answer to his charges," Joyce said.

"I knew I recognized you when you pulled up to the pump. I had to write a letter to your NYPD investigator to explain the charges. That was a long time ago. You made lieutenant, I like that. I am not recording this, let's go into my back room, and you tell me everything, and please start from the beginning."

Joyce told McConville about the night Nate went missing, how and why he went to visit the cemetery and his visit with Carmine Antunnicci, along with reading Mr. Rocco's record logbook. Joyce finished and looked at the judge, who had the same first and last name of his great-grandfather.

McConville had made some notes but waited for Joyce to finish to complete his writing. He took another ten minutes to finish. Once completed, McConville looked at Joyce. "Lieutenant, up here, I have some pull with the trooper's commanding officer." It took the judge another half hour to complete typing out his order. He made copies of it and gave Joyce the original, along with his signature and stamp. A copy for Beth Israel Cemetery and one for the Manhattan DA's office and the defense attorneys, McConville handed Joyce the court orders he needed. Joyce looked at his watch.

"Sorry, Judge, I have to make a call."

Joyce walked out to his car which still had the gas hose connected to the side of his car. He punched in the phone number.

"Would it be possible for you to leave the gates unlocked or leave the key under a brick by the left column or something? I have this strange feeling that I will need to do what I have to do overnight. Thanks. Yes, it will be dinner in two weeks at the restaurant of your choice in Manhattan. No, none of that afterward, sorry," Joyce said.

21

Beth Israel Cemetery Night

Joyce had talked with Carmine, and he remembered that his father had done some digging after midnight, his father always charged extra, so Joyce played with that and hoped for some luck. He didn't need any inquiries about his middle-of-the-night dig. The state assemblyman had so far been kept in the dark, the New York City assemblyman had resigned a year after the case first hit the press after he was caught in a house of prostitution during a NYPD public morals raid.

Joyce had a half hour to kill, so he decided to call Elizabeth. It had been a day and a half since they talked, she was still accustomed to his long periods of silence. He leaned against the side of his Mustang as he waited at the entrance to the cemetery. He had the key to the gate on his key chain which was locked onto his belt. He looked up at the clear sky at the multitude of white dots in the sky. The phone rang four times.

"Hello?" came Elizabeth's tired voice.

"Hey, babe, it's me," Joyce said.

"Who is me?" Elizabeth said playfully.

"Your husband. I left my regular cell in my dresser and took out the battery, just in case the defense or prosecution tried to call me at the last minute," Joyce said.

"Isn't that what you wanted, for them to call you as a witness? You said they didn't need you."

"Liz, normally if the prosecution or the defense talked with me about the case, they would have to inform the judge of the conversation. The judge may or may not want to question me, but since the two teams decided they didn't need me to testify, that freed me up to do my thing, and I am doing it."

"Bob, where are you?" she asked.

"In one of our favorite places," he said. She understood that he was in a cemetery. Its location was anyone's guess, and she understood that. It would take a dinner at her favorite restaurant once the case was over for her to do her shower entrance to their bedroom.

"How is the case going down there?"

"The television reporters say the jury may get the case as early as this morning."

Wow, it is flying by, the last one took five months before it even went to the jury. What the hell is their hurry? Joyce thought.

"Will you be home for dinner tomorrow?" she asked.

"Not sure." He saw three cars and a backhoe approach.

"Look, babe, I gotta go, the military is here."

"Go get them, whoever they are. Have you eaten anything since this morning?" she asked.

The phone went quiet.

Joyce smiled when the four vehicles surrounded his car, it was beginning to get lighter. Two, marked, New York State Police patrol cars and an unmarked State

Police car stopped and turned off their engines. Carmine kept the engine running on the backhoe. His father had not had a mechanic tune it up in years, it backfired every time he turned it off. Joyce motioned for all to approach.

Detective Collins stepped out of his SUV and walked to Joyce.

"Lieutenant, I'll need to read the court order before we proceed." Joyce handed Detective Collins the court order signed by Judge McConville. Collins quickly read the judge's order.

"It looks like everything is in order," Collins said. Joyce walked the detective to the side of the road, out of earshot of Carmine and the uniformed trooper.

Joyce talked softly. "Hey, Tom, how many times have your chops been busted for your name?"

Collins took a step back. "Dad was a bartender on the weekends and he thought it was a cute idea. Up here no one has a clue as to what a 'Tom Collins' is, except maybe some of the seniors. My mother only agreed to it if she had a girl, she would choose her name."

Joyce held his head down. "Not Bloody Mary."

Collins fell to one knee laughing, he quickly recovered. "Elizabeth, my sister's name is Elizabeth."

"That's my wife's name, having said that, I want to have all our i's dotted and t's crossed. Is your forensic expert due soon?" Joyce asked.

"Our guy is creepy, he only works midnights, but he is good. He has agreed to sign a confidentiality agreement on this case."

"Sounds good, let's get digging," Joyce said.

"The gate is locked," Collins whispered.

Joyce reached for his key chain and pulled off the gate chain. He held it out to Collins. “Sharon Rosenberg left it for me,” Joyce said proudly.

“Did she cook you a brisket for it?”

“Not yet, but she wants to.”

“Her brisket is the best but you have to perform afterward.”

“Sorry, I’m happily married.”

“Sharon doesn’t care about that, but I have to warn you, she snores like a trucker.”

“Is that from experience?”

“My wife and I were separated when I met Sharon, after the first night with Sharon, we got back together and have been happily married ever since.”

Joyce smiled and walked to the gates to open them. Suddenly Sharon Rosenberg came up the road. Joyce unlocked the gates and secured them with bicycle chains to the ground poles on both sides of the opening.

“Bobby, what are you doing?” Sharon asked.

“I have a court order which allows us to dig up a specific grave in this cemetery.”

“I thought you were going to visit your relatives, not desecrate a grave. I’m calling the police.”

“Sharon, meet Detective Tom Collins from the New York State Police.”

“Oh yeah, the boom-a-rang boy. One night with me and bam he’s back with his wife.” Joyce wanted to laugh but did his best not to smile, but he did have tears in his eyes.

“I have a court order right here.”

She tried reading the paper in the night light but is unable to. Joyce pulled out a small but powerful flash-light and held it for her.

"It's from Judge McConville and it is for a specific plot. Now you could show us where the gravesite is or we may have to open up a few graves to find it. Then you would have to explain to the relatives of the deceased why the ground was disturbed."

"After I make a call to my assemblyman." She pulled out her cell phone. "It says no service."

"That meteor shower earlier knocked out the satellite service to this area," Collins said.

"I'm sorry, we have to get to the grave, a man's life may depend on it," Joyce said.

"I'm locking the gates once you get inside so you can't get out until I get phone service."

"I cabled them open, so no one could close them, even you."

"Bob Joyce, I thought you were an honest cop when I first met you."

"I am, trust me," he said.

"I did."

"Just think of it as you saving a man's life," Joyce said.

"Oh, by the way, Sharon, Carmine will be digging up whatever his father illegally buried beneath the grave, and it is with his father's permission."

She stood at the gate with her arms folded. "You still need my permission. Damn you, Bob Joyce, I thought you could have been my husband."

Collins turned away as his face reddened. Joyce kept a straight face.

Section F, Row M, Grave 21

Joyce stood near the open grave as the backhoe pulled up more rotted wood and a skull. The simple pine box was in its last stage of decomposition.

"How much further down?" Joyce shouted.

Carmine looked at Joyce. "About an inch, I can see the black plastic," Carmine said.

"Be careful," Joyce shouted over the backhoe's engines. One of the Troopers pulled his cell phone from his belt and walked away from the excavation.

"You got a banana that needs to be peeled. Just throw it in the hole," Carmine said. Joyce understood.

Joyce motioned for Carmine to bring the bucket to him. "I'm going down."

Joyce stepped into the backhoe's bucket as Carmine slowly lowered him into the hole. There was no odor from the unearthed grave.

Decomposition must have ended years earlier, Joyce thought. He could see the plastic bag and the outline of the skeletal remains of a little body.

"Tom, call your guy, we have a body."

"Not without a probable match," Collins said.

Joyce began to brush away the remainder of the dirt, it was dry. He felt the thick industrial waste garbage bags used in the late 1970s, which were not very environmentally friendly. He continued to remove the dirt, exposing the entire bag. He untied the knot which had been tied thirty-seven years earlier. It hid the tragic, fatal family accident. Joyce used his flashlight to examine the contents. The plastic kept the little boy's clothes somewhat recognizable, his hair remained on top of the boy's skull, though the skin was nonexistent. Joyce didn't want to compromise the "crime scene" too much. He just needed to take a photo, but his throwaway phone did not have that option, and he left his mini camera in its charger on his nightstand at the motel.

"Hey, Tom, toss me your cell phone, I need to take a picture of the kid's teeth for a comparison."

"I'll call my guy, we need to maintain this as a crime scene. Why don't you just come up? Oh crap, Bobby, we got company, not good. Get the hell up now," Collins said.

Joyce climbed up the bucket of the backhoe onto the damp moist ground. A tall trooper with an angry look on his face approached.

"That's my major. Someone must have called for him to come out this early," Collins whispered to Joyce.

"Remember, I'm the civilian here," Joyce replied.

"I want this stopped immediately," the major ordered.

"Major, I have a judge's order which allows me to exhume the body in this grave," Joyce said.

"I have a superior court judge who says for you to stop immediately," Major Middleton said sternly.

"I will need to see a copy of the judge's order and your affidavit that you are acting under his/her authority," Joyce said.

The very angry major looked over to Detective Collins. "Detective, who the hell does this jerk think he is."

"Sir, I'm Bob Joyce, a retired lieutenant from the NYPD."

"If you do not stop, I will be forced to have the detective place you under arrest."

"Major, I don't know who sent you here to stop me, but I have just uncovered the remains of a little boy, who was possibly killed years ago in New York City. The assemblyman from this district, how long has he been serving?" Joyce asked.

"Forever. I'm here thirty-five years and he was serving long before that," the major said.

"Major, I doubt you had any intentions of getting involved with a homicide cover-up," Joyce said and held his breath.

Collins interrupted. "He's on his way. He should be here shortly."

That was enough of a distraction for Joyce to call Judge McConville.

"Yes, Judge, the major is here. We are being prevented from continuing. We just need to get a comparison of my copy of Nate's dentist's record and the teeth from the skull. Would you like to speak with him?" Joyce paused for a moment.

"Oh, okay," Joyce said and turned toward the major.

"It's Judge McConville. He's going to call the governor's office. You should be getting a call soon," Joyce said.

The cell phone on the major's belt began to vibrate. The major ignored the call.

"Major, with today's GPS technology, it puts you and me right here at this grave. I doubt if Judge McConville will back down from this issue. We now have the corpse of the little boy from SoHo who went missing back in 1979. I have a copy of his dental records and I am waiting for Detective Collins to give me his phone to take a comparison picture," Joyce said.

The major looked at Collins. "Trooper, if you give him your cell phone to use, you will be in Buffalo by sundown."

"Hey, sweetie, I can help. I use two phones during the day, you can use mine to take a picture or two," Sharon said as she tossed her cell phone to Joyce.

"It will take the pictures you'll need. You can keep the phone until you get to the city. I will wait for the service to return in my other phone," she said.

She never realized Joyce and the major had used their cell phones. Service had just returned to the area. It was an old-type flip phone, which Joyce used years earlier.

"I'll have a brisket waiting when you return it."

The major pulled his cell phone from his belt and sent a call out to the number, then he realized who he was calling. The major turned and walked away from the gravesite.

"I thought you said it would be easy to stop him. He's got more juice than you have. I'm giving him the okay to continue and I will have my troopers standing by to assist with anything he needs."

Joyce looked down, he didn't want the major to see him smiling. The major turned and walked back to the grave. "Continue with what you were doing," the major said.

"Major, that previous conversation we had a few minutes ago, well, it never happened," Joyce said.

A Cadillac Escalade slowly made its way to the gravesite. The driver stepped out and walked over to the major.

"Doc, what are you doing here?" the major asked. He was very surprised that the former Albany forensic pathologist for the previous thirty-five years, who recently retired, had been called out to the crime scene.

"Judge McConville called me and asked me to help the lieutenant in his investigation. I am now the lieutenant's forensic expert," Martin said.

"I just gave him the green light to proceed. I thought you were retired as the trooper's surgeon?" the major said.

"I am, but when a judge asks you for a favor, you do it. Never get a judge mad at you," Martin said. They both smiled and shook hands.

Joyce stepped into the bucket to go back to get little Nate's body. "I just got a call from my wife. I asked her to turn on the service to my phone back home. I gave her a list of phone numbers and people she should look for. A reporter, a friend of mine, called me to tell me the judge was getting ready to charge the jury in the Munoz case." Joyce slid the photo of Nate's dental x-ray, next to the small photo on Sharon's cell phone. "Doc, can you give these a quick scan and let me know what you think?"

Martin looked at the photos from the precinct detective file of Nate's teeth and the skull photo Joyce had taken while in the grave. He repositioned himself to get more light on the two photos. The sun would be over the mountains in twenty minutes but he wanted Joyce out of the area before more calls were made. Collins signaled for the trooper to hand Dr. Martin his flashlight to help. The trooper eagerly complied.

"Lieutenant, the teeth from the x-rays and the pictures from the skull are from the same person. Give me one of the boy's ribs to do a DNA test for absolute identification. I will write a report and send it to you, I will just need your telephone number."

"Six-four-six-five-five-five-four-nine-five-four." A tall man, with a midsized beard, his arms were strong, his eyes were soft blue, he spoke in a very calming voice. "That number is for the telephone the lieutenant is using now, his normal phone is 7-1-8-5-5-5-8-1-2-4," the man said.

"Sir, do I know you?" Joyce asked.

"I believe you do, but sometimes things change. I strongly believe that you should take the little boy's remains with you to Manhattan," he said.

"Have I ever arrested you?" Joyce asked.

"No, but you have called on me from time to time. My name is Larry," he said.

"Why do I know that name?" Joyce returned.

"Billy may have mentioned it."

"Careswell, you know Billy Careswell," Joyce said excitedly.

"He asked me to keep an eye on you. I've been watching you all night."

Joyce quickly looked around for his car, there were none, except for his car, Sharon's car, and the trooper cars.

"I'm better than that," Larry said with a smile on his face.

Joyce took Nate's backpack out of the plastic bag and carefully handed it to Larry. "I would put that in a clear plastic bag if I were you," Collins said.

"I wasn't prepared to retrieve anything," Joyce said.

"I have some in the trunk of my car," Sharon said proudly and quickly raced off to her car.

Joyce was amazed to see how Larry's monstrous arms gently held the backpack of Nate.

Sharon returned with an armful of clear plastic bags and a large "body bag." She pointed to the large plastic bags covering Nate's remains at the bottom of the eight-foot hole. "I think you'll want to put the boy's remains in here with the plastic. If his parents buried him as you say, their fingerprints should still be on the plastic."

Joyce looked at her quizzically.

"What?" she said sternly.

"I watched *Kojak* with my first husband. Telly was my dream cop and a lieutenant at that, and now I am helping a real live lieutenant," Sharon said proudly.

Larry took one of the plastic bags and snapped it open cleanly. He could feel the three books in the small backpack. He knew Nate's name would be on one of the books.

"Hey, Lieutenant, I think you may find some interesting reading from the books inside," Larry said.

"The backpack will go in the trunk of the Mustang along with the boy's remains," Joyce said as he pressed the remote button to his car.

"The backpack can go in the trunk. The boy will never be in a trunk again. I will go with you to wherever you need to go, and I will carry him," Larry said.

Joyce didn't say a word but laid out a few of the clear plastic bags at the bottom of the hole, then he placed the body bag on top of them and opened it. He wiped off as much of the dirt off the original thick plastic bags. He tried not to smudge any fingerprints, if in fact there were any after all these years.

"Lieutenant, I can have my troopers drive you down to the city," Major Middleton said.

"That Red Mustang is mine, she'll do fine," Joyce replied.

"Bob, don't you think you should have the troopers escort you and your car for continuity of evidence? Here is a small lock to seal the bag," Sharon said.

"Where did you learn that, oh, right, I forgot, *Kojak*," Joyce said.

She smiled. "Hey, Bob, when you come back with my stuff, how about a veal-parm hero or a lasagna with sausage," she said.

"Where did a Jewish girl learn to cook Italian food, and with sausage," Joyce said.

"Rosenberg is my married name, my maiden name was Sharon Maria Antonia Puglisi. I kept my married name."

"Didn't you say your uncle left the cemetery to you?" Joyce said as he handed the body bag containing little Nate Zapata's remains to Larry. "My husband's parents were so happy when he married me that they adopted me, so I became their daughter after their son was killed. I just couldn't call them Mom and Dad so they became my aunt and uncle. The name helps up here," she said.

I've been doing ancestry for a long time, and stuff like that makes me want to just sit down with a glass of wine and try to think it through, Joyce thought.

Joyce walked over to the major and Detective Collins. The major spoke first. "Lieutenant Joyce, any relation to Trooper Christopher Joyce?"

"My nephew."

22

The Long Way Home

Joyce looked down at the speedometer as he trailed the lead state police car by twenty feet with the second trooped car followed from ten feet behind. He was doing close to a hundred and five miles per hour. The "on" ramps to the highway had been blocked. The lead car was in the middle lane but turned into the adjoining lanes which made the turns smoother. Joyce had put the top down on his convertible, just in case there was any remnants of Nate's decomposition.

Larry's massive arms were cradling the black body bag as though he was holding a baby. Suddenly Joyce realized that there was absolutely no wind blowing Larry's long hair or rustling the body bag, while his hair was all over his face from the wind.

"Lieutenant, mind if I call you Lieutenant?" Larry asked.

"Not at all, I sort of like it after all these years."

"Lieutenant, how many cemeteries have you visited on you search?"

"My wife and I probably have been to and walked around a hundred to a hundred and fifty cemeteries since we started searching our ancestry."

"How many looking for Nate's remains?"

"About twenty-five."

"How many dinners did it cost you to get the information from a worker in the cemetery's office?"

"Three." Joyce looked to the right side of his peripheral vision as Larry asked the next question.

"How many times did you sleep with those women?"

Joyce was still looking to the side when he answered. "None, and why am I telling you this, you already know the answer."

It was then he realized that Larry was not moving his lips to speak.

"I know, Lieutenant, just trying to keep you honest."

"Larry, I just need to ask you a question. You have been holding those plastic bags containing what I hope are little Nate's remains. There is nothing in those bags except traces of hair and bones, why?"

"I was listening to his heart."

23

Almost There The Zapata Apartment 5:30 in the Morning

Nate's area, in the open apartment, had long since been removed. Arlene and Alan had another child, a girl, to replace him. All memories of their son had been erased from their apartment. Alan had recently dyed his hair brown, as it had gone completely silver. He had kept his hair at shoulder length, but it stopped growing in some areas, so he shortened it for a more conservative look for the press. Arlene's hair was salt and pepper. She refused to cut her long locks, they were mid-back. The couple sat at their table still in their pajamas. Alan's hair with its slight comb-over fell mostly to one side. Arlene's face looked tired as she held her earthen color coffee mug, the last of a set she had been given as an engagement present. The coffee pot finished percolating. She could see the glass bubble at the top of the coffee maker, it was now all dark, the coffee was ready.

"Arlene, this is the second pot of coffee and it is not even seven. We don't have to be there until eleven or possibly not until after lunch," Alan said.

"You snored like an out-of-control truck on one of those mountain roads near your cousin's old house. I kept having the same nightmare; we were sitting on the couch, watching reruns of those comedy shows, like we never left the seventies. Suddenly two men burst into our apartment and arrested us for Nate's murder. They were very happy to put those police things on our hands. We were treated so cruelly by everyone. Even our own defense attorney called us names," she said.

"I had those dreams when it first happened."

"When you killed our son, Nate. Why did you have to hit him so hard that night and across the side of his head? I can still hear the crack when you hit him. Then he fell, hitting his head on the coffee table," she said. She took another sip of coffee to hide her face from her husband's stares.

"When he said he was going to tell his teachers about those four men and what he said those men did to him. I can't imagine how you let your cousin let those bastards abuse our son just so she could supply herself with enough heroin for a week. Arlene, she took him to the lower east side, to those abandoned buildings. They raped our son, every Friday, four men, how could you allow that to happen to our son?" he snapped back.

"You and your stupid picture taking. We had our apartment occupied with little bratty kids all day long. Yeah, I know, you helped me, but at the first excuse, you ran out like your ass was on fire," she said in defense. "I can't understand why I did not believe Nate," she continued.

"I give you that, but please, no shouting. We never know who is listening at our door for the slightest newspaper story," he said.

Arlene walked over to the coffee pot and poured herself another six-ounce cup. She sat back in her chair and waited for her husband to speak.

"Okay, look, my boss was under the gun to make cuts and I knew if the media got news of Nate being abused and that we did nothing, I would have been fired."

"You killed Nate, you hit him and his head hit the coffee table, you did nothing, you put a mirror under his nose to see if he was breathing and nothing. You said he died. You had him buried, where, I haven't a clue. I have never been to our son's grave. I don't know if it even has a grave marking. I have never been able to put a rock on his grave to tell him that I had been there and that I still loved him. I have nothing. You removed everything of his. I have nothing of our son's, nothing," Arlene said.

Arlene started to sob uncontrollably. He tried to wrap his arms around her but she pushed her arms up and cleared his arms from her body. She stood up, walked over to the coffee maker, and poured however slight it was of the coffee into her mug and then went into their bathroom. She looked into the mirror and hated what she saw. She had aged so much since the first day her son went missing. Though never one for makeup when she was younger, she craved for it to hide her wrinkles. Long gone were the skintight jeans, though skinny jeans were the fashion craze of today. She knelt down to the toilet bowl and vomited.

East Side of Manhattan
NYC Medical Examiner's Office

The lead car of their mini motorcade pulled alongside of the medical examiner's office on First Avenue and East Thirtieth Street. Two uniformed officers from the Thirteenth Precinct stood outside the front door. They were surprised to see the red Mustang Convertible, with its top down, in between two New York State marked police cars, their lights were still on. Joyce opened his car door and raced around to help Larry. Larry was already out of the car, standing. He carefully held Nate's remains. An orderly came out with a gurney and Larry placed Nate's remains onto it and covered the body bag with a sheet. One of the troopers handed Joyce a key. Joyce turned to the two police officers. "This is the key that opens the lock to the body bag. Please open the lock and give me the lock and key," Joyce asked.

One of the officers took a step forward and put his hand out for the key. Joyce placed the small key in his hand. He stepped back and opened the lock and removed it. He handed Joyce the key and the lock. Both the NYPD officers and the New York State troopers introduced themselves to each other, then they made their notations. Joyce thought, *Chain of custody has now been completed.*

"Sir, we should start down to the courthouse, they should be returning from lunch. I have heard nothing on the radio as whether the jury has come to a decision," one of the troopers said.

"Nothing over our radio as of yet," Officer Belcastro said.

“Excuse me Lieutenant, does your cell phone accept e-mail messages or photos,” Trooper Harrison asked.

“No, why?” Joyce asked.

“I have just received something from my wife that you may want to look at.”

“Could it wait until we get to the courthouse?” Joyce asked.

“I have a friend, a court officer at the courthouse who is working the trial. It should be waiting for you when you get there,” Harrison said.

Joyce walked back to his car. Larry had already opened the car door and sat in his seat. He grabbed the shoulder harness and buckled himself in.

“Larry, do you want to see what a New York courtroom looks like?” Joyce said innocently.

“Been there, done that,” Larry said without looking at Joyce. He adjusted the shoulder harness over his chest.

Joyce thanked the two NYPD officers and waited for the New York State troopers before getting into his Mustang.

Hallway to the Judges’ Chambers
111 Centre Street
1410 Hours

The troopers agreed to return the body bag and cell phone to Sharon Rosenberg. Joyce cautioned them, as they were both single and perfect fresh meat for Sharon. Joyce waited nervously in the hallway, a court officer stood with Joyce and Larry. He questioned the necessity of Larry’s presence in the courtroom.

Joyce heard the three low raps on the wall by the court officer. The judge walked into the courtroom only to ask for a short recess. The defense, Billy Careswell, and the prosecution team looked at each in wonderment. Joyce's phone began to vibrate. He didn't recognize the caller's number.

"No need to answer it," Larry said.

Joyce lowered his head a little. "Mr. Rocco died, didn't he?" Joyce said.

The judge returned to his chambers and talked with the senior court officer for a few seconds. It was time to see the lieutenant.

The large oak door opened and a white shirted court officer leaned out of the door. He looked at Joyce and Larry. "Lieutenant, he wants to talk with you . . . only."

Joyce looked at the officer and then to Larry, who shrugged his shoulders.

"I want Larry inside with me."

The door closed and quickly reopened.

"Why do I feel like I'm Dorothy waiting for a meeting with the wizard?" he whispered to the court officer.

The officer wanted to laugh but kept his composure. "He can come in with you, but he can't say a word," the court officer said. He handed Joyce a sheet of paper. Joyce quickly looked it over, folded it and put it into his rear pocket.

Judge Ruttenberger sat behind his desk, in his tall leather-back chair. He recently had his hair cut. He wore a bright white dress shirt under his robe. The bright light from his shirt would make him appear to be younger. "Lieutenant, you have been under the radar for some time now."

"Well, Judge, I had been interviewed by both the prosecution and the defense regarding my involvement in this matter. I recently asked both sides if they needed me to testify and they both responded in the typical way. No . . . sorry and . . . thank you, we will not be needing your testimony," Joyce said.

"Lieutenant, could you briefly tell me what you said to the lawyers about that night?" Ruttenberger asked.

"Well, Judge, it started on . . . ," Joyce began.

Joyce finished by showing the Judge the white sheet of paper. Judge Ruttenberger quickly read it and returned it to Joyce. "Lieutenant, you certainly have all your bases covered when you come to court."

"Judge I always did during my time as a cop, sergeant and even as a lieutenant, and I am so glad for this final piece of information," Joyce said.

24

Telling the Truth In the Hallway, Outside the Courtroom

The door to the courtroom opened slightly. Judge Ruttenberger never looked up as he talked with the jury. Joyce and Larry walked into the back of the courtroom and stood against the back wall, as all the available seating was filled. Larry stared straight ahead at the Zapatas, Joyce as usual looked around the courtroom for the reporters. There was a slight mumbling and Judge Ruttenberger quieted the courtroom with a rap of his mallet, but not before Arlene Zapata turned around to see Joyce and Larry. She quickly turned back around and crouched into a ball.

"What's the matter?" Alan whispered at his visibly distressed and nervous wife.

"Jesus, they're here," Arlene said.

"Who is here?" Alan asked.

"The two men in my dreams, they are here, in the back of the courtroom," she said.

Alan turned around and saw Joyce and Larry standing at the rear of the courtroom. Judge Ruttenberger again snapped his gavel onto the wooden stand.

Joyce turned to Larry. "She pegged you right away." Judge Ruttenberger recognized Joyce's voice and only raised his gavel. The courtroom was now in total silence.

The court officer called out to the jurors, "Ladies and gentlemen of the jury, have you reached a unanimous verdict?"

"Yes, we have," the jury foreman said.

The foreman handed a sheet of paper in an envelope to the court officer who in turn handed it to the judge. The judge opened the envelope, read the contents, then he placed it on his desk to his right.

One of the court officers at the door to the courtroom opened the door and stepped out only to return seconds later. He whispered something to Joyce. Joyce nodded his head and stepped out of the courtroom with Larry. Ruttenberger continued.

"Sorry Lieutenant but I had to come into the courtroom to see the end of the trial, Trooper Harrison said. Joyce pulled out the sheet of paper and held it as though he was reading it for the first time.

"Trooper Timothy Harrison, any relation," Joyce asked.

"My dad. I never looked at his records or reports that they gave to my grandfather at my mom and dad's funeral."

"What happened to them," Joyce asked.

"My dad was a Trooper and one of his zones encompassed Beth Israel Cemetery. It wasn't until you were talking about the night Nate Zapata went missing this morning, did I make the connection. My dad always worked the midnight tour so he could be with me when my mother went to work as a nurse. They had planned their vacation in Niagara Falls for a year. It was supposed to be a second honeymoon as my mom got pregnant with me on their first night of their honeymoon. My grandparents agreed to take care me for the long Memorial Day weekend. I was two years old at the time, so I don't remember anything, only what my grandparents told me. My father was working the night the boy supposedly went missing, but he was so anxious to go away with my mom that he brought home his paperwork from work that night. My maternal grandmother, wanted to burn all the paperwork, but my paternal grandfather demanded that he safeguard the paperwork until I was old enough to comprehend it. It would be my decision whether to keep the paperwork or destroy it. It seems that my father had a police scanner in his car that received trooper calls throughout the state. My mother, according to my granddad, allowed my dad his fun and they listened to the police scanner on their way to their second honeymoon. They were almost to the Canadian Boarder when a call went out that two men had shot and wounded a trooper at a local convenience store. My grandfather told me this after my grandmother died. My dad knew the route the perps would take and he waited for them. According to trooper reports and my grandfather, my dad tried to stop the perps car with his car but the perps turned into his car instead of trying to avoid the crash. The crash killed my dad, mom and sister," Harrison said.

"Where did your sister come into play in this," Joyce asked.

"My mom was three months pregnant according to my grandmother. It was supposed to be their second honeymoon."

My grandfather hid all my father's paperwork, especially the reports from his last tour. About a year ago, I was cleaning out my hall closet when a box fell and out came all my father's police paperwork. Stuff my father kept and never filed. I went through all the paperwork and separated my dad's last night on patrol. That is when I came across his "stop" of the car at the cemetery gate on the morning of May 25th. I never made the association but there it was, the name Alan Zapata. My dad's description of the guy as having very dirty nails, a flowered shirt and jeans. My father noted he was kind of stinky."

"That's Alan," Joyce said. "He better fess up in there," Harrison said. "I'd like you and your friend to come into the courtroom and when I call you, could you do a little cop routine and play like you are going to arrest the Zapatas," Joyce said.

"We would love to help, Lieutenant," They shook hands and Joyce returned to the courtroom.

"Will the defendant please rise."

Fausto Munoz stood with his back bent slightly over. He didn't want to hear the verdict nor did he want to spend the rest of his life in jail. Billy Careswell placed his hand on Munoz's shoulder. The Zapatas glared at the defendant's side of the courtroom, almost gleaming. Judge Ruttenberger got the attention of the court officer at the rear of the courtroom and slightly leaned his head down. No one was watching the judge, as all eyes were on Munoz. The rear door to the courtroom opened and Joyce, along with the two troopers, and Larry walked into the courtroom. Munoz turned and see the troopers walk slowly into the courtroom. He fell back into his chair and folded his arms onto the table and began to sob uncontrollably. Two court officers positioned themselves behind Munoz. Careswell leaned over to his client and whispered something to him. Munoz stood up but continued to sob.

Judge Ruttenberger continued. "Let the court reporter note that retired NYPD Lieutenant Bob Joyce, two New York State troopers, and Mr. Joyce's friend Larry have entered the courtroom."

Everyone, including the Zapatas, turned to look in Joyce's direction. Joyce caught Karen Callucci's attention. He mouthed the word "guilty." She nodded *yes*. Joyce walked over to the Zapatas, who were seated directly behind the prosecutor's table, on the aisle. Joyce stopped at the railing and turned around to face the Zapatas as he leaned against it.

"Alan and Arlene Zapata, for nearly forty years, you have had the police and the public throughout the country looking for your son. Your son, who you say you allowed to go to school alone, for the first time, at the age of six," Joyce began.

Alan Zapata stood up, but was quickly brought back down to his seat by Carlucci as she leaned back over and pushed him down with her strong arms. He talked from his chair.

"Your Honor, we have heard all the evidence against the defendant, Mr. Munoz," Alan pleaded.

"Mr. Zapata, please remain quiet," Ruttenberger ordered. A court officer positioned himself between the defendant and Alan Zapata.

"Well, Mr. Zapata, I have a little bit of information about that day. The day your little Nate went missing," Joyce said.

"Your Honor, we know Mr. Joyce's theory but it has never been proven," senior trial prosecutor Hal Whithers said from his table.

"Mr. Whithers, this should be interesting for you. Lieutenant, please continue," Ruttenberger said.

"Mr. Whithers, for the record, I was in your office, and you interviewed me, with your two detective investigators, about what I did that night, the night Nate went missing. You questioned my memory until I showed you my NYPD memo book for that night."

Joyce paused for a moment and pulled out his light blue memo book and held it up for everyone to see.

"I showed you the contents of my memo book by referencing my entry for the night and time my unit, the NSU 2, responded to West Broadway and Spring Street. I presented you a copy of my memo book entry, as I did with the defense's investigator, after he and I had a lengthy discussion of the case. In both incidences, you and the defense's investigator asked me the same two questions. They went like this, 'Lieutenant, do you believe that Fausto Munoz kidnapped Nate Zapata that May morning?' and my answer was *no*. Then you asked me a follow-up question, 'Lieutenant, what do you think happened to Nate Zapata that morning?' I found it interesting that you and the investigator leaned back in you seats and waited for my response, almost in the same manner. My response shocked you, but not the investigator. I said, 'I believe that Nate Zapata never left his apartment that morning alive.'"

There was a collective groan from the courtroom. Judge Ruttenberger gently tapped his gavel once. The audience quieted.

"I gave your office a courtesy call to see if you would be needing me to testify at this retrial of Fausto Munoz and I was told politely, 'Thank you for your interest in this case, but we will not be needing you to testify.'"

"I asked the same question of the defense attorney, I also received a polite, no, thank you." Joyce stood up for a moment, looked over at Larry, and smiled. He returned to the railing.

"I did a little work on my own. I am a licensed private investigator in both New York and New Jersey. Troopers, could you please stand closer," Joyce asked.

The three people sitting next to Arlene stood up and walked to the back of the courtroom. The tall, burly troopers were now each standing next to Arlene and Alan.

"Alan, say something," Arlene pleaded.

"Mr. Zapata, do you know Beth Israel Cemetery in Upstate New York? There is only one. I checked," Joyce said.

Alan Zapata's face went white. "I believe I do." He began to sweat.

"Mr. Zapata, do the names Assemblyman Cowan, Joshua Levy, Sharon Rosenberg sound familiar?" Joyce asked.

"No," Alan replied nervously.

Billy Careswell began to feel a chance for Fausto.

Joyce looked at the judge. "May I continue, Judge?" Joyce asked.

"Proceed."

Joyce looked back at the courtroom audience and not at the judge nor the jury nor the defense nor prosecution table.

"Here's what happened that night." Joyce stopped momentarily and looked down at the Zapatas. "Arlene and Alan, I want you to interrupt me any time I say something that you believe to be a lie. Please do not hesitate to stop me when you believe I am lying."

Joyce began. "The two of you were sitting around your table about to eat dinner. Nate's older sister was over a friend's house for a 'study party.' Nate came from his bedroom area in his Elmo pajamas as he normally did and sat in his chair at the table."

Alan's and Arlene's heads snapped up to look at Joyce.

Joyce hesitated for a moment as he knew he had hit a nerve with the pajamas. He continued. "Nate again requested to be allowed to go alone to his school bus and when he returned after school, and again you refused. Nate continued to protest, this time a little more loudly, unusual for your son. Alan Zapata, you got mad when your son stood up from his chair at the table. You ordered him to sit but he refused to, until you allowed him to go to the bus stop that Friday morning alone. Then the ultimate demand from your son. He told you that he was going to tell his teachers that you, his father, allowed those men to hurt him. He was going to tell that to a policeman he knew. Alan, you got out of your chair and angrily walked over to your son and hit him with the back of your hand. Nate fell, hitting the side of his head on the edge of your coffee table and then he slammed his head on the solid concrete floor. He lay helpless and you never tried to help him. You panicked, you put a mirror under his nose to see if he was breathing and he wasn't. Alan, you never even checked to see if your son had a pulse. You let your son die, because you wanted him dead. Arlene, you ran into your room as Alan began to wrap Nate in two plastic bags. Alan, you called your cousin Joshua Levy so he could quickly and quietly bury your son. Your wife wanted nothing to do with disposing of her son," Joyce said.

Alan looked down at the floor. *How could he know?* Alan thought

Joyce caught Arlene's stare and held it with his eyes. Her body was shaking.

"Arlene Zapata, your cousin let four men rape your son, every Friday, so your cousin could support her drug habit. That is why your husband wanted to quickly bury your son. Alan knew the medical examiner's office would find the anal scarring in your son's rectum," Joyce said. "Mr. Zapata, you no longer have the look of confidence you had that night. Remember, I was there that first night."

Joyce took two steps back and looked at the couple. "Troopers, cuff her," Joyce asked. The two burly troopers gently grabbed Arlene's arm and lifted her out of her chair.

She pleaded with her husband. "Alan, please, tell them the truth. I don't want to go to jail, please."

Joyce interrupted her, "Mrs. Zapata, your husband doesn't have to admit to anything. This is Trooper Harrison, standing to your right," Joyce began. Trooper Harrison nodded his head gently as his non-shooting hand held her wrist. Joyce held out the white sheet of paper for Arlene to read. She was stunned when she read her husband's name.

"That's right Mrs. Zapata, your husband Alan met Trooper Harrison's father, then a New York State Trooper, while he waited for the gates to Beth Israel Cemetery to open on the morning of May 25, 1979." Alan Zapata closed his eyes and bowed his head. Arlene snapped her head to the side to look at her husband. "You never told me that you were confronted by a Policeman," she said. There was no sound in the courtroom, everyone was now fixed on Arlene's next words.

"Trooper Harrison's father and mother were killed in a vehicle accident shortly after he finished his night shift as a State Trooper. His paperwork regarding his service call of a suspicious person at the cemetery was never submitted, otherwise your charade would have been exposed immediately. His paperwork was discovered a year ago and only brought to my attention a few minutes ago.

"All right, all right, let my wife go. I did hit our son, he fell, it was an accident, I swear," Alan said.

There was a low rumble of conversation in the audience. Ruttenberger quickly snapped his gavel. Six members of the press quietly but excitedly walked out of the courtroom. They wanted the interview of the year with Joyce.

Judge Ruttenberger intervened. "Mr. Zapata, I am going to ask you a few questions for the record. Do you agree to answer the questions honestly?"

"Yes, Your Honor, we do," they said collectively.

"Mr. Zapata, did you strike your son which caused him to fall and die?"

"Yes, I did," Alan reluctantly replied.

Larry opened the courtroom door and walked out, Joyce smiled. Billy Careswell wrapped his arms tightly around his client. Munoz stared blankly at Joyce. Carlucci and Whithers stared at each other. Their guilty conviction just went out the window.

"Mr. Zapata, did you illegally bury your son in a grave at Beth Israel Cemetery?"

"Yes, Your Honor, I did."

"Mr. Zapata, did you file a police report which caused alarm never heard so far and wide across this country?"

"I think I did."

"I believe this is the first time something like this has ever occurred in my courtroom. The prosecution will charge the Zapatas with the death of their son, they will be defended by the defense, and the defendant will go free immediately. Case dismissed. Lieutenant, in my chambers, *now*."

Judge Ruttenberger's Chambers

"Judge, what was the verdict?" Joyce asked.

"Guilty."

"Hey, I made a dramatic ending to a tragic story," Joyce said.

Ruttenberger sat at his desk and looked at Joyce. "Lieutenant, you saved a man from going to jail for a very long time. I would have sent him away for the rest of his life. Just one thing."

"Sure, Judge," Joyce said.

"Do you have any of those PBA cards I can put in my car window?"

"I got one better, I have the lieutenant cards."

"By the way, where is your friend Larry, he seemed like a very interesting person to chat with," Ruttenberger asked.

"He must have received an urgent call, you know how Angels of Mercy, they help people."

Ruttenberger sat for a moment, then he stood up and walked over to Joyce.

"Lieutenant, thank you for all you have done for justice. Just one more thing, did you shake Larry's hand, and if so, I would like to shake that hand of yours."

Joyce thrust out his right hand and the judge eagerly accepted it.

"Lieutenant, after all the dust settles, say in a month or two, give Judge McConville a call. He may have some information about your family that you will be very interested in."

Epilogue

Joyce's House

Elizabeth poured herself a glass of red wine and a glass of white for her husband. She was in a robe and had kicked off her slippers as she put her feet on her husband's lap.

"I can't believe you drove down here with the little boy's remains on the front seat of your Mustang. You have a name for her, Anni," she said.

"Well, there was this guy who was a Vietnam veteran and he needed a ride to his lawyer's office. I let him tag along and hold Nate's remains. He sat quietly holding the body bag, like they were his child's remains."

"Oh, by the way, do we know anyone named Larry beside my brother?" Joyce said innocently as he stood up and walked into the kitchen to pour himself another glass of wine.

"Not that I know of."

"He talked about Georgie, the guy you dated before me."

Elizabeth got up from the couch to fill her wineglass again.

"Please don't mention this guy Larry ever again," she said as she finished her glass and refilled it. They stood together in the kitchen, her robe mysteriously fell from her shoulders to the floor.

"Now I know how Lois Lane felt when she learned Superman's identity," Joyce said as he kissed his wife.

"What?" she said.

The End